I0683804

THE SILVER CIRCLE

by Kyell Gold

This is a work of fiction. All characters and events portrayed within are fictitious.

THE SILVER CIRCLE

Published by FurPlanet Productions
Dallas, Texas
http://www.furplanet.com

ISBN 978-1-61450-064-3
Printed in the United States of America
First trade paperback edition:

Cover art by Kamui

CONTENTS

CHAPTER 1 1

CHAPTER 2 11

CHAPTER 3 22

CHAPTER 4 30

CHAPTER 5 35

CHAPTER 6 41

CHAPTER 7 52

CHAPTER 8 71

CHAPTER 9 78

CHAPTER 10 92

CHAPTER 11 106

CHAPTER 12 114

CHAPTER 13 129

CHAPTER 14 135

ABOUT THE AUTHOR 140

ABOUT THE ARTIST 140

Chapter 1

In the reflection of the round silver ceiling lamp, Valerie's face looked unnaturally pale, set off by her short black hair and the smear of blood on her hand, on the tissue she was holding to her nose. She closed her eyes and wondered how this day could possibly get any worse. *Has anyone else lost a husband and a job all in one day? Maybe I'm having a brain hemorrhage, too. That'd be the big three.*

The guest chair in Martin's office was more comfortable than Valerie's desk chair. Martin tapped on his keyboard while she stared up at the ceiling light. Probably a quick note to HR. *Val Creighton verbally abused and threatened a superior. Recommend...* what?

The warmth in her nose felt better, though she had no idea how to tell whether her nose had stopped bleeding. Cautiously, she lowered her head and dabbed at her nose with the tissue. It felt better, and no new blood appeared on it.

"All better?" Martin asked without looking up.

He was in his mid-forties, about ten years older than Valerie, with a round face and receding hairline, though the thick mop of hair behind it was either poorly placed plugs or a terrible toupee. Valerie looked past him out the window. Sometimes she saw deer in the meadow behind the office, but today it was empty, uniform and dark under the cloud cover. "I think so," she said. She didn't know what to do with the bloody tissue.

Martin finished his e-mail and looked up at her, finally. She had absolutely no idea what was coming. She could be fired, or maybe let off with a warning, or asked to go home and have her nose looked at. But whatever he was going to do, she wasn't going to apologize. She already regretted having said that when he was holding her head. She wasn't sorry.

"If I'm fired, just tell me."

He shook his head. "No, no. We like having you around. I realize that everyone's been working hard lately, but I hadn't realized how much stress everyone was under. The kind of outburst you had in the meeting—well, I shouldn't ever let tension get to that point. So I'm willing to take some responsibility for that."

Her outburst would have been a lot more effective without the dramatic nosebleed at the end of it, she thought. "I appreciate that."

"Regardless," Martin said, "there are more professional ways to express your frustration. Obviously the stress has been pretty bad on you."

She couldn't stop the words from spilling out. "Steven brought the papers by this morning. It's final." A thought occurred to her. "When I said I wanted to…with the papers…I wasn't really yelling at you. I think I was yelling at him through you."

He raised his eyebrows. She couldn't tell whether he bought the half-lie. "Why haven't you said something to me before?"

"I told you we were separated."

"But you said you hoped to work things out." His smile might have been intended to be sympathetic, but it came off as more of a leer.

"I tried!" She took a deep breath, and lowered her voice. "I was trying."

"There's no magic wand, with stuff like this." He sat back. "You should've come to me. I'm a good listener."

"I didn't want it to affect…" The words trailed off as she realized how ridiculous they would sound, given how much the divorce had already affected her job. "It didn't affect the work I did on the proposal. That was good."

"Not arguing with that. Bill just put together a better package." Martin gave her a patronizing smile. "I know how excited you were about getting your first billion-dollar client solo. But we've got Vodotech in the pipeline. You might have a shot at them."

"If I do the same thing I did here? Play the game? I did everything you told me to. Except grow a penis."

He laughed, but the smile disappeared. "I never said anything like that. You're a beautiful woman and we all appreciate—"

"You invite me to coffee but not to go out drinking. You talk to Bill and Don about sports and TV shows, but when I show up it's just work, work, work. It's discrimination."

"We've been through this," he said quickly.

"Well, it's not fair." She exhaled, staring down at her hands. There was a small streak of blood at the base of one fingernail where she hadn't washed thoroughly. Should she bring up the fact that Bill was dating Martin's daughter Julia? She'd only overheard him talking about it; she wasn't supposed to know. "It's not fair."

"You know, if you'd like to discuss your thoughts on Vodotech at length with me, I'd love to hear them." He let her get her hopes up before adding, "Say, some night at Trattoria Lupe?"

She'd known this was coming, though she'd hoped he would have the decency to wait until she wasn't holding a bloody tissue. "Why don't I set up a meeting? Sometime early next week. I think I should take a couple days off to clear my head." She tried to laugh; it came out horrible and forced.

Martin coughed and looked back at his screen. "So I sent Donna an e-mail."

Donna was the company's HR manager, a pinched woman who was exactly the opposite of every round, jolly HR manager Valerie had worked with previously. And yet, despite the "wicked witch of the 3rd floor" jokes that went around the office, Donna could be surprisingly sympathetic. As long as you didn't embarrass her by telling other people about it.

"I think, and Donna's approved, that you should take a couple weeks' leave to get yourself together. You can use your five sick days for the first week, and the second week will just be without pay."

"You're forcing me to take a week of vacation? And all my sick time?" Red anger stirred in her again.

"Not vacation." He put his hands up hastily. "Leave without pay. If you want to use vacation time, that's fine, but Donna said you only have a day built up, and the company is very strict on that."

"So strict you let Bill take a week when he'd only been here three months." She forced herself to unclench her fist.

He measured her, then leaned forward. "This isn't about Bill. Look," he said, "you want to play bullshit games, play bullshit games. You're lucky you're not being let go. Screaming? Threatening me? You know, there are a lot better ways to get ahead."

She stared at him. "Such as?"

Martin leaned back in his chair, giving her another smile. "I just had an idea. You know, with the divorce being final, you probably don't want to spend two weeks just rattling around your house. I have a cabin upstate on Lake Wahya that you can use, free of charge. It's beautiful up there. You can clear your head and get a grip and come back ready for action."

"Your lakeside cabin?" Martin talked about it every summer. Valerie had tried to convince Steven that they should buy a lakeside cabin somewhere. He'd agreed and then done nothing, just like with the other things she thought they both wanted.

"I'll have the key couriered over to your place this afternoon. And hey, if I can shake free this weekend, maybe I'll come up and join you." He read her reaction and held up a hand. "There's separate bedrooms. I'll be a gentleman."

"I don't know." She looked again at the empty meadow outside. Getting out of the area sounded really good. She wanted to forget not only about the job, but about Steven and everything else. And her mother would be calling, she knew that.

Martin shook his head, his confident smile returning. "Go up to the cabin. I promise, this whole thing will seem much less important after a couple weeks of R & R." He snapped his fingers. "You know that poster you have up in your office? 'Aliens'? Well, if you like horror movies…" He made a gesture that was supposed to be dramatic. "There are wolves up in the woods there."

Aliens was science fiction, but she let it pass. Steven had said worse and less accurate things about that movie. Wolves were interesting enough, if less threatening than Martin himself. But if he did come up to the cabin, she could go out into the forest. There were plenty of ways to hide from people up in the woods. "All right," she said, finally. "Thanks."

"Thank me by getting better. I just want what's best for you." He wagged a finger at her. She didn't point out that the fatherly gesture didn't go with the Don Juan act. She just smiled and left.

The envelope that arrived that afternoon with the key also contained a map. The exit off the highway was carefully marked, as was the turn off the main road that led to the village where the cabin was. The cabin itself was circled with a little star next to it. That Martin had gone to that much trouble touched her, somehow. Yeah, he was a bit overbearing and he came on too strong, but he'd been divorced for five years. Maybe he was just desperate.

Would she be like that in five years? In five weeks? She traced the route to the cabin with a fingernail. Martin was successful, after all, and he wanted to be with her, which was more than she could say for any other man she knew. So maybe, if he showed up at the cabin, maybe she wouldn't hide right away.

While she packed, she couldn't get the image of rats fleeing a sinking ship out of her mind. Her love life, her professional life, everything was going to shit all at the same time. The dog bed in the corner, the drafts of the rejected proposal all over her home-office desk, the cardboard box marked "S" because she couldn't bring herself to write out the bastard's full name, all of that she avoided looking at as she threw clothes into her suitcase. Steven had taken the rest of the matching set.

She stopped for a fast food lunch on the way, a dry chicken sandwich on bread so soft it might as well have not been there. That plus the fat, salty fries kept her going so that she was only a little hungry five hours later when she pulled up to the cabin in the last fading light of the sun.

This was not an isolated cabin in the woods. It was a cabin in name only, a tidy little one-bedroom house in a small cluster of similar cabins, on the western shore of a narrow lake near the south end. The nearest cabins, barely visible from her front door, were little more than dark shadows among the trees. No cars sat in their driveways, no lights burned in their windows. So she was isolated, even if the cabin wasn't.

The key turned smoothly in the lock, letting her into a chilly foyer with several boring landscapes hanging on the walls. The lights all worked as she walked around the cabin, exploring the modern kitchen (garbage disposal and dishwasher), living room (50" plasma TV), and bedroom (42" plasma TV, terrible hunting lithographs, and condoms in the nightstand drawer). She ended up out on the deck looking over the lake, the row of house-shaped shadows like dark, jagged teeth on the reddish reflections in the water.

"Couldn't afford a west-facing house, eh, Martin?" she murmured. Or maybe he just didn't like sunsets. Figured he'd be an early riser. Thought of himself as a young go-getter. "I hate people like that," she said, and then looked to the right and left to see if any of the neighbors were out watching her talk to herself.

The adjacent decks were empty, but when she looked to her left, she saw, on the opposite shore of the lake, a flicker of fire in a patch of darkness. It went out and then flared to life again, for all the world like an eye winking at her. The sun was sinking quickly, but she was fairly sure she hadn't seen any buildings over on that side. Maybe there was a campground there, a place where she could get away from the getaway if she needed to.

With the key, Martin had given her a small binder with all the rules for guests at the cabin. Among the cautions she skimmed was an address for the general store, open until seven daily, with the added instruction that she should "go meet Leon as soon as possible." Despite her current inclination to do the opposite of whatever Martin told her, she would need to get some basic supplies if she were going to be here for two weeks.

The general store, unlike the cabin, looked exactly as she'd pictured it: a small house whose lower floor held brightly lit, widely-spaced shelves of produce and groceries, and whose upper floors were undoubtedly where Leon and his family stayed. Leon looked the part just as much: a sturdy man who might have once been a lumberjack, his white beard neatly trimmed, his red flannel shirt clean and buttoned nearly to the top. He was bagging groceries for another customer, a tall, thin man with salt-and-pepper hair, wearing white pants and a white leather bomber jacket that looked too thick for the warm season. She heard them talking as she walked by, something about taking kayaks out on the lake again, but Leon looked up from the conversation to wave cheerfully and say, "Evening, miss."

It had been years—the better part of a decade—since Valerie had been called "miss." She allowed herself to glow, shutting up the part of her brain that told her it hadn't been meant as a compliment. I'm on vacation, she told herself, and that means I can enjoy insincere flattery for once. She waved back to him. The customer gave her a sharp look and then picked up his bag.

He wore a silver ring on his left hand. Valerie wouldn't have noticed it except that her hand went unconsciously to the bare spot on her ring finger when she saw it, and then she realized that it wasn't on his ring finger. He wore it on his middle finger. She thought that odd, but then, people wore stranger jewelry in stranger places, back in the city.

She filled her basket with instant dinners, and selected a few cuts of beef and some chicken breasts, figuring she'd feel more ambitious later in the week. On vacation, she reminded herself when her brain tried to stop her from reaching for the package of Pecan Sandies. I'll run it off, or swim it off, or...or I won't, and I won't worry about it.

"Amazing how Pecan Sandies can make you feel like you're on vacation," she told Leon when she came up to the counter.

"I love 'em," he said, and patted his midsection. "That and butter pecan ice cream."

She found herself smiling. "Not an every-day treat, though. I'm Valerie. I'm staying in Martin's cabin, 670 Kiskaton Drive."

"Welcome to Sycamore Heights Estates, Valerie. I'm Leon." He held out a tan, callused hand.

"Martin told me about you," she said. "I'm just here for a couple weeks. What's good to do in the area?"

"Lots," he said. "What do you like to do?"

A motorcycle pulled up outside the store, its throbbing roar muffled, then dying. "Anyone rent bikes?"

"Sure," he said. "There's a dirt bike place up the road. The best trails are up on the north end. But you don't wanna ignore the lake."

She'd meant motorbikes, but she didn't correct him. "I'm not really good around water. Isn't that what everyone comes here for?"

"We're between seasons, so it should be kinda slow. There's kayaking on the lake. Even if you've never done it, it's easy. You'll get the hang of it right away. You can rent one up at the Rec Center, that's up the road, turn toward the lake, make a right, you'll run right into it. You here by yourself?"

She hesitated automatically, but his manner was so genial that she didn't feel the need to lie in the otherwise empty store. "Yep. Just a getaway from work." And then, because she couldn't help herself, "I'm going through a divorce right now."

He nodded sympathetically. "Like I said, we're between seasons. Summer and winter, there's dances and dinners, if that's your kind of thing. But there's plenty to do on your own, too. Lessee, you can go hiking. Some great trails up the mountain."

The door jangled. A tanned young man with raven-dark hair and a sharp nose slouched in. His dark eyes scanned Valerie, and then he turned and wandered over to the beer cooler.

Leon tensed up immediately. He didn't take his eyes from the young man. "Course," he said loudly, "you want to be careful. Take your husband with you whenever you go out to the wilderness."

Valerie opened her mouth to remind him she was here alone, but he went on. "Not always safe to wander around alone," he said, still staring at the young man, and she understood then what he was doing.

"I'll remember," she said. She couldn't resist a curious look at the young man as Leon finished ringing her up. He was paying them no attention at all, standing at the beer cooler holding the door open as though he were comparison shopping, one hand holding the door, the other in the pocket of his black leather jacket. Except that he was just staring at the beer without doing anything, the same way, Valerie thought, that she'd been staring at the frozen dinners in the supermarket that first day after Steven left her. She hadn't been looking at them at all; she'd been wondering how long she could stand in the cold before she got numb.

"You need me to walk you to your car?" Leon asked.

"I'm okay," Valerie said. The day she couldn't handle a few young punks...besides, the kid by the beer seemed to be alone. She couldn't see anyone out front. And she didn't want Leon to have to leave the kid alone in the store, even for a moment, even with the big glass windows he could see through from the parking lot.

"You have a good evening, then, and come back tomorrow and let me know how it was." He turned his full attention on her for the span of the good-bye, a big, genuine smile and a handshake. But as she walked out the door with her groceries, he yelled at the kid, "Hey, pick something and close the door. This ain't a library."

She had to giggle at the thought of a beer library. She put the groceries in the back seat, and then looked around to try to find the vehicle the young man had driven. He looked like the motorcycle type, for sure, but there was no motorcycle in the parking lot. In fact, her car was the only vehicle. So maybe he'd walked over. Must live nearby, and that would make sense, given that Leon seemed to know him well.

And there weren't any other kids hanging out in the parking lot, or anywhere along the way back to the house. So he was on his own there. What harm could he get up to? Leon was certainly capable of looking after the store.

Tonight wasn't the night for chicken or beef. Tonight was instant dinner night. She poured the mix into a saucepan, added water and milk, and turned on the heat. For good measure, she tossed in some tuna fish. The smell brought back her college days, before she had the husband and the important job and every meal had to feel like a Family Meal. And that thought brought her back to the young man in Leon's store. Was he still in college, or just out of it? Or never went? She hated to indulge in stereotypes, but this didn't seem like an area that sent a lot of its children on to university.

She took the meal out to the living room and resisted the temptation to turn on the TV. The sun had set, but the stars were dancing on the lake, the moon was nearly full, and the air was refreshingly cool, so she took her meal out to the deck and sat, the simple food pairing well with the quiet, simple night.

The drawback was that the food got cold quickly. She had just begun to wonder whether she wanted to finish the rest of it or reheat it in the microwave when she heard a crunch from somewhere off to the right of the deck. She sat very still and listened. Of course, she thought, there'd be raccoons around, and other wildlife, and here she was bringing food out into the open. And not just any food, but artificial cheese sauce, which she was pretty sure you could smell a mile or so away.

It had sounded heavier than a raccoon, too, like something big stepping on twigs. Martin had mentioned wolves, but they were just like big dogs, right? Were there mountain lions in upstate New York? Mountain lions and wolves were supposed to be light on their feet—or paws—and wouldn't have made that crunching noise. Were there bears? She couldn't remember, but suddenly the fact that she hadn't heard anything after that one step was making her nervous. The light spilling out from the windows of the living room suddenly made her feel like a sitting duck, and the darkness filled itself with creatures climbing the deck, waiting just outside the light to seize their moment to pounce.

She stood, pushing the chair back with a loud scraping, and walked quickly into the living room. Her heart was pounding for reasons she could barely fathom. She tossed the dish in the microwave, but didn't press any buttons. She'd only heard one footstep, which meant that whatever she was listening to had tried to be silent, and that implied that it was stalking her.

But that was ridiculous. It was clearly just after her food. Idiot city girl, bringing food out onto the deck at night. She left the room-temperature tuna in the microwave and walked back to the closed patio door, turning out the light on the deck on her way. Pressed with her nose to the cool glass, she scanned the woods beyond the deck, now silver-brushed in the moonlight.

"Of course Martin would have told you if there were dangerous wild animals at the cabin," she murmured. "It would've been on the instruction sheet." Her voice echoed in the silence of the house. She would go turn on some music, she decided, and crawl into bed.

She lingered at the glass a moment longer, then another. Try as she might, she couldn't shake the feeling that something just beyond her field of vision was watching, waiting for her to leave. Okay, this is silly, she told herself. I'm going to—

Something moved. A shadow, just on the other side of the deck. She stared, waiting for it to move again, heart pounding so loud she could hear it in her ears, a wild, savage rhythm of panic. There *was* something out there. It was that shadow right there, the one now holding perfectly still. Something was out there. It had moved like a bear, not like a wolf or a mountain lion. Like something upright, swinging an arm across the deck.

And now it was standing still, that shadow right there. Or had it been that one? Or the one next to it? They all looked the same now.

Her heart slowed. Had she even seen a shadow move at all? She laughed uncertainly. "You're scaring yourself, Val," she said. "Time for a glass of wine and a good night's sleep."

Even though the sheets on the master bed smelled clean, she changed them for spares she found in the closet. With a glass of wine from the pantry and a book from her suitcase, she curled up in bed. But though she was always able to lose herself in a book, the shadow lurked around the edges of her mind.

Maybe that young man from the grocery store would have been able to protect her. He looked well able to handle himself in any situation, unlike many people she'd known who wore ostentatious leather jackets. There was a look to him, a rough confidence, that wasn't very common in the city, or at least not in the office environment she was most familiar with. Leon hadn't liked him, but if he'd been truly dangerous, Leon wouldn't have let him in the store, would he?

Look at her, fantasizing about the leather-coated rebel. Well, what harm would it do? This was supposed to be a vacation, after all. And thinking about him coming into her room, slowly taking off the leather jacket, coming to the bed…it drove the shadow from her mind. She fell asleep with the light on.

Chapter 2

She'd initially thought she would go on a hike, but the shadows of the previous night lingered in her head, and she decided she would be safer on a kayak on the lake. Ten minutes into her first voyage out, she laughed at herself, wobbling through the lake. "Safer, maybe, but not drier," she muttered, but with a grin. After another ten minutes, she had the hang of paddling and felt more assured that she wouldn't capsize the small craft.

The other two kayaks on the water, piloted by a middle-aged couple and their teenage son, slid gracefully as swans past her, up the lake. In the time she'd gotten less than halfway to the small island in the middle of the lake, the other two kayaks had shrunk to specks at the far end. Valerie put the paddle away until they were well past her, pretending to lounge back and enjoy the sun, which had come out from behind the clouds.

Out here on the lake, the air was chillier, but with the sun on her, she was warm enough to leave her denim jacket open. Her cotton shirt breathed nicely in the cool air. If she looked away from the marina where dozens of sailboats were tied up, past the wooded island to the far shore, she could pretend there were no other people on the lake.

Sadly, she couldn't lie back and drift for long without itching to go somewhere. There were no other obvious destinations, so she set out for the opposite shore of the lake. At least if she crossed it and came back, she'd feel she'd accomplished something. Her clumsy paddling took her past the island, a small area about half a mile long dotted with trees whose leaves were just beginning to turn. Might be a nice site for a picnic, if she'd thought to bring a lunch. Maybe tomorrow.

The idea that she had nothing to do tomorrow, nor the day after, nor the next twelve or thirteen, made her paddle faster, which did not actually make the kayak go faster, though it did increase the amount of splashing. Well, she would have a picnic on the island tomorrow, she decided, and then the day after, she would hike. And if it rained, she would stay in and drink wine and watch movies.

She'd just cleared the island, halfway between it and the far shore, when a noise like a growl made her turn her head. So she was looking directly at the island when she heard the cry of a man, cut short by another snarling growl.

The shapes from her deck the previous night seemed to loom in the shadows of the island. When a man dressed in white staggered out from the trees clutching his throat, she jumped. He fell to his knees, gasping for breath with wheezes so loud she could hear them across the forty yards of water that separated them. Then, understanding what she was seeing, she dug her paddle into the water as fast as she could, turning the kayak in a circle before managing to point it toward the island. She looked across the water for anyone else to call to, but the other kayaks were still specks at the north end of the lake, and otherwise it was as serene and empty as it had been the whole morning.

While she struggled toward the shore, the man fell to his side. The wheezing stopped. She paddled harder, panic giving her strength, and some twenty yards out, she fell into a rhythm that moved her along the water. A brief flash of triumph at having figured it out was swamped by worry and fear as she watched the prone figure. In another minute, she was near the shore, and she realized that she had no idea how to get out of the kayak successfully. But the man was lying there, helpless.

Her paddle scraped bottom. The rocky shore didn't offer any easy place to steady the kayak, so she just grabbed one of the outcroppings and pulled herself onto the rock. Without giving any thought to the untethered kayak, she climbed down the rocks to where the man was lying.

It was the salt-and-pepper-haired man she'd seen in the general store the night before. He was wearing the same white bomber jacket and white jeans, and an empty quiver slung over one shoulder. But the grass and dirt under his neck was stained red, and so was the hand he had pressed to his throat, the silvery ring on his middle finger catching and reflecting crimson streaks. Above his hand, his Romanesque features looked grim and determined, rather than afraid. She knelt beside him, and gently lifted his hand aside.

It resisted, sticky with blood. Valerie gritted her teeth and pulled, and the hand came away abruptly, sending her sprawling backwards. She ignored the pain in her wrist, because she couldn't take her eyes from the shredded ruin of flesh that lay glistening in the sun. Blood trickled from it down the collar of the jacket and onto the ground.

The cinnamon rolls she'd had for breakfast roiled in her stomach. She turned to the side and vomited onto the grass. There's nothing you can do for him, she told herself, but she couldn't allow herself to just walk away. Even if he's dead, you need to try to find his ID, or something. And maybe he's not dead.

Avoiding the sight of his neck, she crawled closer and picked up his hand. It was still warm, but no matter where she pressed on the wrist, she couldn't find a pulse. His jacket was open, so she reached up and pressed her hand against the flannel shirt where his heart should be beating. She felt nothing there. When she reached back down to his hand again, it was colder.

Oh, God. She forced herself to look at the throat. It was torn, definitely torn, and now that she was close, she saw long tears in the front of his shirt, just where something's claws might have dug in while its teeth were tearing him.

She turned away, breathing evenly against the churning in her stomach. Just look for his ID, she told herself. Please God let it be in his jacket. She patted the exposed jacket and felt a bulge where there would be an inner pocket. Reaching inside, she found a slender wallet and a folded piece of paper. Her hands were shaking as she opened the wallet. The name on the International driver's license was Anton Vojacek, and the home address was a mass of accented consonants that she presumed belonged to some Eastern European country. The only other contents of the wallet were an American Express Platinum card in the same name and about a thousand dollars in hundreds and twenties. She set it down and unfolded the paper.

In an old, neat hand was written "Lake Wahya," and below it "ten male, eight female." Below that were directions that she recognized as the same ones she had followed up from the city, an address, and three phone numbers, all with the local 607 area code. Across the bottom, in a hasty scrawl that looked far more recent than the other writing, was the phrase, "old pine stand, white rock." He probably had a cell phone on him somewhere, but it wasn't in one of the jeans pockets she could see. Likely he was lying on it. She didn't feel up to turning him over, so she put the wallet and paper into her hip pack and stood up.

Only then did she become aware of a rustling in the woods that was too strong and constant to be the wind. Of course, whatever animal had done this to him must still be on the island. Adrenaline surged through her, sending her stumbling back to the top of the rocks and down the other side before she realized that her kayak was floating peacefully some fifteen yards away from the shore.

She could swim, but she wasn't sure she'd be able to get into the kayak on the open water, let alone make it to the other shore. Wildly, she scanned the lake, but her kayak was the only one visible. Nobody was walking around on the opposite shore, where she'd seen the fire last night. And of course nobody else was on the island. She turned back to the woods, heart pounding, waiting for the animal to emerge.

She saw it first as a shadow on all fours, and thought it was a small bear. Then it looked too small to be a bear, and she thought it was a wolf. But it rose to its hind legs, staggering toward her, and she thought it must be a bear again, until it came out of the trees and she recognized the young man who'd been in Leon's the night before.

He was holding his right hand inside his black leather jacket, which swung free around his bare chest. Whatever'd got Anton must have gotten him, too, but at least he was still breathing and able to walk. She clambered down from the rock and ran around the corpse, toward the young man, relieved to have an excuse to look away from the body. "Hey," she said, "what happened? Do you need help?"

He looked up at her, his eyes wide. He wasn't as young as she'd thought, she saw. The leather jacket and motorcycle in the parking lot had been deceptive. Up close, he looked to be her age or maybe a little older, in his mid-thirties. She had her hand extended as she approached, but rather than taking it, he pushed her shoulder. She could tell it was weaker than he was expecting, but it was still enough to send her stumbling away. "Get...fuck...out..." he panted, and dropped to his knees by Anton's body.

His breathing was labored. He couldn't take his hand from his side. Clearly, he was injured, but if he didn't want her help, then...but no, she couldn't just—"Hey!"

He had tried to pick up the body. Failing, he was now pushing it along the dirt, toward the rocks at the edge of the lake. She ran over and grabbed his hand. He pushed her again, but this time she was ready for him and she pushed back. He spit at her, "Don't...fuck around..."

"What?" She stared.

He faced her, finally. His eyes were a deep liquid brown, black hair dripping with water or sweat. She saw now that his belligerent defiance was speckled with fear. Of course, he'd just been attacked by an animal. But the odd thing was that he seemed to be afraid of *her*. "Do it or stay the fuck out of my way."

"Do what?" She couldn't look away from his eyes. There were flecks of gold in them, she saw now, as though a light were shining through behind them.

His eyes flicked down to her left hand, and then he relaxed. In a quick motion, he pushed his arms under the body and lifted it off the ground, but only tottered forward a few steps before grunting and dropping to his knees. The body fell to the ground against a large rock as he pressed his hand to his left side again. "Bastard," he breathed.

"You can't just dump him in the lake," she said, taking a step toward him.

He held his side, hunched over, his face twisted in pain. "Apparently not," he said. "You gonna help?"

"No! Jesus, we need to call the authorities, and you need help, too. We've got to get you to a hospital." Anton's throat gaped up at her. She pushed down the hysteria. "Did you kill...whatever attacked you?"

He went very still, and shook his head.

"Then it's still out there. We need to get off the island." She looked again at the small shape of her kayak, bobbing some twenty yards away. "How did you get here?"

"Swam," he said shortly. He lifted his eyes abruptly to stare at the far shore.

She followed his look, but saw nothing there, just the thick trees and the shadows in them. "You both swam?"

He shook his head, then fell to his knees, trying once more to push the body toward the rocks. Fine, Val thought, go ahead and die, crazy man. But she took two steps toward the shore, staring out at the kayak, and then back at him. The savaged flesh of Anton's throat rose in her mind, an image she wouldn't soon forget. This leather-jacketed biker, already wounded...if she left him, he would certainly die, too. She imagined blood streaming down his handsome face, and flinched.

But if they hadn't both swum, then Anton had had a kayak, or a canoe, and hopefully he'd been better about tying his up than she had. So there was a way to get back.

She strode back and grabbed the man's left arm, resisting his attempts to shake her off. "Leave me alone," he growled.

"You...need...help." She gritted her teeth and pulled harder, until he cried out and doubled over. She let go, afraid she'd gone too far, but he struggled to his feet.

"This doesn't concern you. You should...stay away." He winced, bending forward and then straightening again.

"Don't be so stubborn," Valerie said. "We can both get out of here. We both should get out of here."

He stared at her, their faces inches apart. There was moisture on his lips as they parted, then closed again. Valerie could feel heat coming off him in waves, the heat of exertion and maybe fear. She wondered what it would be like to kiss him. Jesus, she thought, it really has been too long.

"I'm not going..." He tilted his head as though listening, though the lake was completely still. Then he turned to her and gestured to the north end of the island. "His canoe is over that way. Come on." He strode past her and was halfway down the beach, moving with surprising speed, before she could react.

"Hey!" She ran after him. "Why didn't you tell me that to start with?"

He shook his head again, his right hand still holding his left side. His breath was coming in long, harsh gasps, but it didn't seem to be affecting his stride. Even with his injury, she couldn't get closer than fifteen feet behind him, barely able to follow him when he dove between the trees.

She hesitated. But the sound of his footsteps growing fainter was the only noise she could hear. Whatever had attacked him and Anton was either on the other end of the island still, or resting. And the man—whose name she didn't even know—was charging fairly recklessly through the brush as though he knew he wasn't in any danger. She stepped into the brush, following the noise he was making.

He seemed to know his way around the woods. Probably he was a naturalist of some sort, riding his motorcycle around to different parks. The glimpse of his chest she'd caught through his open jacket looked more firm than she'd have expected from a scientist, though it was certainly hairy enough, so maybe he was a hobbyist. And he and Anton had been here to try to catch a glimpse of a bear, and had gotten too close and it had attacked them. So he was trying to hide Anton's body so that nobody would know the bear had killed him and nobody would come hunting it?

That was weird, but as Steven had liked to say, in the city you see weirder things than that walking to your car in the morning. There were animal fanatics around, for sure. Come to think of it, that might also explain why he wasn't wearing a shirt under his leather jacket. One of those "become one with the wilderness" kind of people, she'd bet. No wonder the bear had attacked him.

That made her feel oddly better. The image of a peaceful bear being provoked to attack by a couple of amateur nature-lovers allowed her to go a little slower through the woods, until she saw the lake through the trees ahead of her and heard splashing.

She hurried forward, emerging onto a rocky beach in time to see the naturalist-biker sitting in a canoe tethered to a small tree. He was holding a long, narrow case; as she watched, he threw it into the water. "Cast off," he said, pointing at the tree. "Then hop in."

Now she could hear the putter of a boat engine, in the distance. "We should wait for the patrol," she said. "They'll be able to get you to a hospital faster."

"It's not the patrol," he said. "Come on, I need your help."

She frowned. The engine noise grew louder. "Who is it, then?"

Fear rose in his face. He sank down into the canoe. "Just cast off, already!"

She thought at first that his wound was bothering him, but though he was still holding his side, he was peering over the gunwale of the canoe out at the vast blue expanse of the lake. He lifted the paddle and tried awkwardly to lever it over the edge. Doubt flickered across her mind—why was he afraid of the patrol? And then: what if he's right and it isn't the patrol? The engine noise, coming from the hidden side of the island that faced the marina, was growing louder.

She walked quickly to the tree and unfastened the simple knot. Holding the rope, she looked back toward the shore where they'd left Anton's body. She should wait here for the authorities. Fleeing the scene of a crime was a crime itself, she thought. Or maybe that was just car accidents. At the very least, it made her look guilty, if anyone had seen her on the island, or would see her leaving it in the canoe.

Then he pulled the paddle back into the canoe and turned from his study of the lake to look at her, his chin resting on the side. His face was twisted up in pain or fear. "Listen," he said, his voice hoarse. "I can't go by myself."

She still hesitated. With an effort, he said, "Please." His eyes looked right into hers.

Valerie took one more look back to where the body lay, and then dropped the rope and ran for the canoe. She splashed through the shallow water and clambered in. "Give me that," she said, grabbing the paddle he was holding. He was also clutching an Indian-patterned blanket, which he now pulled over himself until only his face was showing.

"Don't talk to anyone on the lake," he said. "And don't look at me."

He covered his face. Valerie pushed the canoe away from the rocks and hissed, "Where should I go?"

"Doesn't matter," came the muffled reply. "Somewhere safe."

She dipped the paddle into the water and pushed, sending the canoe away from the island in a wobbling line. Somewhere safe? She'd been at Lake Wahya less than twenty-four hours. The only safe place she knew was Martin's house, and she wasn't about to drag a complete stranger in there. "I'll head for the car," she said. "There's a hospital a few miles up the road."

"No hospitals." His voice came sharply through the blanket.

"You're hurt—"

"I just need a day or two. Don't talk any more. Sound carries on water."

The paddle had a sticker marking it the property of the same place where she'd rented the kayak. She pushed for the marina, thinking about her kayak floating somewhere over near the other side of the lake. She'd have to tell the man at the rental place—Hanley, was it? Or Henry?

The buzz of engine noise drove the question from her mind. She looked to her left and saw a small motorboat coming toward her, a man standing in the prow. He slowed when he saw her, out of courtesy, she thought at first, but as his sharp blue eyes fixed on her, she wondered if he'd slowed to get a better look at her and her canoe. He stood tall and muscular, his white hair like a lion's mane in the breeze from the lake, and he looked familiar in a white blazer and slacks. She stared back at him until she saw a glint on the middle finger of his left hand and realized that he was reminding her of Anton Vojacek.

She looked away quickly, focusing her gaze on the marina and struggling to paddle toward it. Though the canoe was easier to steer than the kayak had been, the wake of the boat now made it swing back and forth, every stroke she took pushing her in a different direction. And still, the man in the motorboat drifted closer; where the sound of the engine had made her nervous before, she found herself pleading silently for it to start up again. In the silence, she could feel his eyes on her, accusing her of murdering his brother.

His brother? Where had that come from? But she was sure it was right; Anton was this man's younger brother, and for some reason, the guy in the front of the canoe didn't want to meet him.

Well, it stood to reason. He'd just seen Anton mauled to death, and probably didn't want to deal with explanations now. But she felt for the older Vojacek, too, out looking for his brother. She should tell him—what? "Did you have a younger brother? Because I just saw someone who looks like you with his throat ripped out back on that island there." She shuddered, not wanting to revive that mental image. Not to mention the fact that he'd probably ask her to come back to the island with him, and she wouldn't be able to explain why she couldn't.

At least she could wave to him. That would be more natural, wouldn't it? She looked up, arm raised, to find him barely twenty feet from her, still staring directly at her. The smile froze on her face. His severe expression didn't change at her gesture, nor did his eyes waver. He was not, fortunately, looking at the blanket with the wounded man beneath it, but she almost wished he were.

He was drifting still closer. Her heart raced. What the hell? She had no reason to be threatened by him. "It's my first time in a canoe," she said. "Sorry. I'll get out of your way."

He didn't react at first. Then a wide smile broke over his face and he inclined his head. "Do take your time," he said. "My apologies."

His Eastern European accent was not a surprise, though his English was perfect. He kept his eyes on her as she pushed the canoe forward, until she'd passed the boat and couldn't see him any more. Still, the engine puttered quietly, making her imagine him following the canoe at a safe distance. Sweat dripped down her forehead.

The marina didn't seem to be getting any closer. She paddled as hard as she could, and then, blessedly, the motorboat's engine revved to life. Its wake pushed the canoe along as it powered away, toward the farther shore.

"You did good," her passenger's voice came to her, a muted baritone. "Thanks."

"Who is he?" she asked. "And for that matter, who are you?"

Apart from the persistent background buzz of the engine, the lake was silent. "My name's Breaker," he said.

"Breaker? Like the surf?"

A corner of the blanket curled back so he could frown at her. "Like trailbreaker," he said. "What's your name?"

"Valerie," she said. "Valerie Creighton—Michaels." She kept her eye on the marina, forging ahead.

"Valerie Creighton-Michaels? Of the Syracuse Creighton-Michaels?"

"Just Valerie Michaels." She glared at him.

He smirked briefly, then leaned his head back to look up at the sky. "So, Valerie Michaels, what does bring you to Lake Wahya at the end of the summer, when there's nobody around but us locals?"

"Getting away from it all," she said, panting from the effort of paddling. The marina was getting closer. "Jesus, what happened back there? What attacked you?"

He stared up at the blue sky. His body shifted, under the blanket; she guessed he was holding his wound again. "It's a dangerous world," he said.

"Was it a bear? I don't know what else could have…" The vision of Anton's ruined throat superimposed itself on the marina. She shuddered.

"Wolf could have," Breaker said.

She drew a picture from horror movies, a large, slavering beast, prosthetic jaws dripping with blood. "We're almost there. Just another few minutes."

He didn't answer. In the bright sun, his face retained its dark tint, and with the raven hair, she wondered whether he were Native American, not just tanned. But then, a Native American wouldn't be so stupid as to lead someone else into a bear attack, would he? Or was that racist of her, assuming he was an experienced woodsman? Mocking her misspoken surname as a pretentious hyphenation felt like the attitude of someone who'd seen a lot of TV, or read a lot of books. Maybe he had been hired on the basis of his heritage and had screwed up, badly. That might explain his eagerness to run away from the scene, his fear of Anton's brother.

They were almost to the marina. Instinctively, she steered away from the place where she'd rented the kayak, to a small patch of quiet shore. Her car, if she recalled, was parked not too far from there, and unless there was a fence, it would be a short walk through the woods. She preferred that to trying to explain why she was helping a wounded man out of a boat she hadn't rented.

But as it turned out, she didn't have to help him much at all. As soon as the canoe scraped bottom, he threw the blanket off and swung himself over the side. He landed in the shallows with a splash and dropped to his knees, grunting.

"Wait!" she called, stowing the paddle, but he was up on his feet again, forging up the beach. As quickly as she could, she jumped out herself and ran to his side.

"What the hell is wrong with you?" she yelled. "What, are you going to just go curl up under a tree and eat grass 'til you feel better?"

He stopped. "Thank you for your help," he said. "You don't owe me anything. Enjoy your vacation." He paused. "I hope you get away from it all."

"Don't be a macho asshole," she said, grabbing at the edge of his jacket. "If you're not going to a hospital, you're going to need to get that wound dressed somewhere. Where's your home? I'll drive you—"

She stopped, staring at his exposed left side. A broken wooden shaft protruded from an angry red puncture wound, just below his ribcage. The slender wood buried in his flesh was gruesome enough, but in addition to that, the skin around the wound had erupted in an oozing rash.

He yanked his jacket back from her. "It's none of your concern," he said.

"You've been shot." With his jacket hanging open, she could see now that there was a similar rash in a line just under his collarbone, an angry red welt only partially hidden by the fine black hair on his chest.

"Stabbed, actually." He turned away from her.

She clutched his jacket again, pulling him half out of it as he tried to get away. "Okay, I've had just about enough of this! I save your life..." He glared at her. "Yes, I saved your life. You can't swim off the island, you can't paddle a canoe—you would've starved to death."

His lips pressed together thinly. "You know nothing about me."

"I know you were in a fight," she shot back. "I know there was an animal on the island, and it killed Anton. But it didn't hurt you, did it? *He* did." He didn't say anything. "And his brother is out there looking for you."

"Yes." His voice had dropped to a low growl.

"So go to the police. Tell them he attacked you."

"The police," Breaker snarled, "brought them here."

Chapter 3

She stared at him stupidly. "They brought him here? But not to fight you, right? That—that must have just happened."

He gestured at the wound in his side, wincing at the motion. "Yes. We were having a nice conversation about the fall migration, and then his arrow just happened to slide out of his hand."

"But…"

"Valerie." He was breathing heavily. "They brought him here to do what they can't. That's all. Go back to your happy world where the police protect you and strangers don't wait in the shadows to kill you. And stay out of the woods. I don't want to see you get hurt."

"Why would I…" She trailed off, seeing again the piercing stare of the man in the motorboat, the ruin of his brother's throat.

Breaker's gold-flecked eyes met hers. Not angry, just serious, and maybe a little worried. "Call the police if you must. You can even describe me. You won't be telling them anything they don't already suspect. But stay in your cabin, stay out of this fight. You're not made for this."

He started to walk away again. She yelled after him, "Who *is*?"

To her right, she could hear the noise of people on the marina. Faintly, ahead of them, a car approached and then passed them on what must be the Lakeshore Drive. He braced himself against a tree with one hand, the other still pressed to his side, and turned so that she could see his sharp profile against the dark tree bark. "We are."

It would have been easy for the words to sound arrogant, pretentious, like a Chuck Norris action hero. But to Valerie, there on the shore of the lake, they sounded tired, resigned. She stared at his profile. "Who's... we?"

Breaker exhaled. He started to walk again, slowly, deliberately, through the trees. Valerie took two steps after him and then stopped, watching his shadow meld with the woods.

Good riddance, she told herself as she stomped along the lake shore to a small hill from which she could see the marina. Just another man who thinks he knows what's best for you. To hell with him anyway, and his crazy stories about the police.

Her car was parked on this side, and there was a chain-link fence surrounding the complex, she discovered. She walked all the way around it until she got to the entrance, and then had to walk along the street, where there was no sidewalk, until she reached the parking lot. At the car, she remembered that she had to explain where her kayak was.

She rubbed one hand through her hair, wet with sweat. Screw it, she decided. I'll call them later this afternoon and make up something. It felt rebellious and dangerous, and after a day of wild animal attacks and some kind of deadly-contract-killer-versus-Native-American-tribe Tony Hillerman drama, that was about as dangerous as she felt she could handle.

The clock in the car told her it was 11:54. Somehow, that didn't seem possible. But even by the time she'd driven back to the house and flopped down on the couch in the living room, it wasn't even 12:30. How do you follow up a morning like that? She laughed, shortly. Martin had been right about one thing, at least: her marketing proposal seemed a whole lot less important now.

The reassuring normality of the cabin already made the dead man and Breaker seem like part of a dream. If not for the fact that her head was still damp with sweat, she might almost feel she'd fallen asleep on the couch and dreamed it. The fabric of the couch smelled of leather cleaner, and even when she turned her head to press her nose into her shirt, the smell of the lake was faint. But as faint as it was, it recalled, like a flash, Breaker's profile. So dark against the sky, so light against the trees. Curiosity scratched at her mind, but she closed her eyes firmly and lay a hand over her face.

The restless feeling wouldn't go away, and she was starting to feel hungry. She should at least take care of the kayak, while she was avoiding thinking about the rest of it. Best to get it over with and find out what she was going to owe them.

Focusing on that made it easier to leave behind the memory of Anton, his brother, and Breaker. She made a sandwich for herself and walked out onto the deck with Martin's cordless phone. "Hi," she said between bites when Sammy from the rental counter answered. "I rented a kayak this morning and…uh, I landed on the beach, and got out to walk around, and when I got back the kayak was gone. I guess it just floated away." That was mostly true. "I just got back home and…I mean, what do I do now?"

Sammy laughed. "It's no problem," he said. "The patrol picks up floating kayaks all the time. Just, if you wouldn't mind, can you come back down to the rental office and sign a 'lost craft' form so we can match the one you rented to any that they find?"

"Sure. There's no charge?"

"Well," he said, "if they don't find it in a week, we'll have to charge you for the cost of the boat. But they always find them."

"What's the cost of the boat?"

"It's fourteen hundred dollars." He sounded almost apologetic. "But I'm sure they'll find it. In fact, they might even have found it by the time you get down here. I'll radio them and ask."

"Thanks." She finished the last bits of the sandwich and looked out over the lake, but she could only see the family she'd seen earlier that morning. No patrol boat, no floating kayak, no elder Vojacek on his motorboat. And no Breaker. Her eyes drifted down to the woods between the house and the lake. She could hear animals moving around, but nothing that sounded large enough to be a man. Or whatever had been around last night.

Her skin prickled. She stepped back inside and closed the patio door. She'd go down to the kayak place, deal with the form, and ask the guy if there were anywhere she could rent movies. Something British with flouncy dresses and witty dialogue and romance would be perfect. She could open one of the bottles of wine Martin had in the kitchen and just relax, forget about the crazy morning.

She weighed the phone, staring out at the lake through the glass door. Should she call the police? In the city, the one time she'd seen a car accident happen, it was on a busy street and literally a dozen people had their phones out calling 911 before she had a chance to reach into her purse. Here, though, she might be the only one for days who knew Anton was dead.

Her and Breaker. And Anton had tried to kill Breaker. So Breaker should be the one to report it to the cops. And if he didn't…if he didn't, well, she could rent a kayak again tomorrow, paddle around by the shore, and "discover" Anton's body. That sat uneasily with her, but it was enough that she put the phone down without dialing.

On her way down, she drove past a truck, a black pickup that she only noticed because it reminded her of Steven's. It was going slowly down the narrow road, and when she glanced up at the driver, she saw with a shock that it was the elder Vojacek. He didn't see her, so intent was he on scanning the forest on either side of him. He was looking for Breaker, she knew, and she found herself almost laughing. Did he really think Breaker would stroll along the road?

But as she drew alongside him, the urge to laugh died down. The silver-haired man was staring at the woods with feral intensity, as if he were looking directly through her. She felt with a shiver that he could see through the trees as well. Then he was past, and the feeling was gone. She glanced in the rear view mirror at the truck crawling along the street, then set her eyes forward.

Sammy, a weathered man with a military crewcut and an easygoing smile, reported that they hadn't found the kayak yet. "Where exactly did you leave it?" he asked.

"On the island," Valerie said without thinking.

He gave her a curious look. "How'd you get back, then?"

She flushed. "I met a man there…he gave me a ride on his canoe."

His curious look faded into a grin. "Oh," he said. "Nice private place, the island."

It took her a moment to catch his meaning. "It wasn't that," she said, but she could hear the defensiveness in her voice and knew her protestation wasn't helping.

"Ain't none of my business," he said, and put the form down on the counter. "Sign here. You want me to call when they find it?"

"Sure, thank you." She surveyed the form and then scrawled her name at the bottom. "Say," she said, "any wild animals on the island?"

His grin returned. "Just the usual. Squirrels, 'coons. Foxes when the lake freezes. Why?"

"Nothing like a bear?" She remembered Breaker's words. "Or a wolf?"

At the word "wolf," his grin vanished. "No," he said. He stacked the paperwork and filed it under the counter. "No wolves on the island, and they ain't dangerous if you stick to the lake or the trails anyway."

Valerie frowned. Why would he assume she thought wolves were dangerous? Did she look scared? "Are there many?"

"Some." His expression lightened. "Sorry, ma'am. It's just been kind of a problem. We make our living off tourists, y'know."

"I thought tourists would like wolves." Though the sun was still bright outside, the office had a curious chill to it now.

Sammy just shrugged. "They don't know how to behave," he said. "Sorry, there's some people coming back. I should go give 'em a hand. Anything else you need, just give a call, and I'll let you know when they find that kayak."

"Okay," she said. "Thanks." But he was already moving out from behind the counter, over to the dock.

Jesus, she thought, walking back to the parking lot. Freaky area. Standing by her car, she looked through the fence at the trees. Was Breaker still out there? Well, that was his business, not hers. He'd made that clear.

But still, on the drive back, she found herself slowing through the wooded area, glancing from one side of the road to the other. Just in case, she told herself. She rounded a bend in the road and there, pulled off to the right, was a black pickup truck, gleaming in the dappled sunlight.

She slowed, passing it. The cab was empty. Now she looked for a silver mane in the shadows and patchy sunlight, but the only motion she saw was of furtive shadows, the flitting of birds and the scurrying of small animals through the trees.

Not your problem, she repeated to herself. Not your problem. She rounded another corner and turned into the lane that led up to Martin's cabin. As she turned the key in the lock, she heard a polite cough behind her. She turned to see the silver-haired Vojacek standing politely, some ten feet behind her.

"Do excuse the intrusion, please." His voice was accented, Eastern European with a little British English behind it as well, like many of the wealthy foreign investors who'd come through their office in years past. From this distance, she could see that he wasn't as old as she'd initially thought. His hair, smooth and well-kept, must have gone prematurely grey. Perhaps he was the younger brother after all. "I recognize you. From the lake, you remember?"

She nodded, not trusting herself to speak. His smile seemed completely natural, as though he really had been charmed by her out on the lake.

There was no reason for her to be as wary as she was, except for that same feeling she'd now gotten twice around him, the feeling of knowing something about him that she couldn't possibly know. He went on. "I am in pursuit of a man. I saw him in the woods near here and then lost him."

He paused, allowing her a moment to say something. She remained silent. "This man is a criminal." Now his smile vanished, his face growing more severe. "I have enlisted the help of the police, but I would very much like to apprehend him myself. He is a young man, with unkempt black hair, a little shorter than I am. He likes to keep to the shadows, and is often seen wearing a leather jacket."

So he'd already called the police. Breaker's story gained some credibility in her mind. Maybe both brothers were working with the police, and the police were corrupt, somehow...

The silver-haired man was looking at her, and she realized that he was waiting for her to acknowledge his words. "What's he done?"

The blue of his eyes recalled glacial ice more than blue sky. "I would prefer not to alarm you with details," he said. "Suffice to say he is wanted by the police."

She nodded. "How can I help?"

The smile returned. "I simply wanted to ask if you had seen him, and if not, if you would take one of my cards." As if by magic, he was holding out a small business card to her with his left hand. His silver ring gleamed on the middle finger.

She reached out and took it. It was cold, as though it had been sitting in the air-conditioned glove compartment of a car all morning. "Anton and Karol Vojacek," the card read, and under it a phone number and the single word, "Professionals." She felt Anton's wallet weigh heavily in her hip pouch. Why hadn't she taken it out? Karol was still smiling at her, but she felt the creeping sensation that he could feel his brother's wallet, that it was reaching out to him somehow. "Are you Anton or Karol?" she asked.

"I am Karol. You may encounter my brother Anton as well. I would ask you to extend to him the same courtesy you do to me."

Hide you behind some boulders? She repressed a hysterical giggle and nodded. "How will I know him?" *He'll be the one with the giant gash in his throat.*

Karol smiled. "Everyone who has met us has remarked on the resemblance. I will be surprised if you do not recognize him."

She held the card, not daring to open her hip pouch to put it in. "I'll keep an eye out," she said.

"One more thing, Miss..." He waited for her to fill in her name.

"Creighton," she said. "Val Creighton."

"Miss Creighton." She didn't correct the 'Miss.' The way he said her name, very deliberately, made her feel as though he had reached out and taken her hand in his. "This man is very dangerous. Do not engage with him should you see him. Lock yourself in the house and call me." He looked appraisingly at her. "You are an attractive young woman, and he can no doubt be charming. I trust you are intelligent enough to keep yourself safe."

"Thank you," she said, and he bowed stiffly, then turned and walked back down the lane.

She waited until he'd rounded the bend before opening the door, reluctant to expose the inside of the house to his eyes should he turn around. When she did slip into the house, she locked the door behind her and immediately took Anton's wallet out of her hip pouch. She held it in one hand, standing in the entrance to the living room beside the phone. Of course she should call the police about it. But what possible explanation could she have now for having it and not having turned it in earlier? *I found it in my driveway, officer. No, it was just there.*

Lame. She walked into the kitchen and pulled open one of the drawers there, stashing the wallet behind the sharp knives. Slamming the drawer shut felt good in a way, relieving her of a responsibility, but it also felt uneasily like sweeping a problem under the rug. She knew she'd only have to deal with it later.

"We'll deal with it later," Steven always said, and her argument, "why not deal with it now?" went unheeded. The problem was that she couldn't quite figure out how to deal with the problem of Anton's wallet now, except to do nothing. When his body was eventually found, they would just assume that someone had stolen it. They might try to trace the credit card, but since she wasn't about to use it or the cash, she didn't have anything to worry about. She'd take it out and drop it in the lake, maybe when she went to "discover" Anton's body.

As tidy as that solution was, the wrongness of it still gnawed at her. Was she the kind of person to help cover up a death? And a death with all these questions lingering around it, no less? Breaker knew something more about Anton's death, she was sure, even if he hadn't said so directly. What if, she thought again, he'd caused it somehow? Guided Anton out to the island and into the lair of a bear, or a wolf?

If Anton had been hired by the police, along with his brother, that gave Breaker plenty of motivation to get rid of him, assuming Karol was correct and he was wanted by the police. And he'd made her, Val, a party to his crime.

This was all pretty fucked up. There was no reason she had to stay in Martin's cabin, except that it was free. She could head up to Buffalo and stay in a cheap motel somewhere, or take a week to drive back home, staying in roadside places along the way. As beautiful as the lake was here, probably it was best she didn't stick around, with wild animals and dangerous criminals roaming around, and things going bump in the night on her deck.

Tomorrow morning, she'd pack up and head out, somewhere. The decision made her feel better, calmer. With a Diet Coke from the fridge, she walked out into the living room, took one look at the patio door, and screamed.

Chapter 4

Blood trickled down the patio glass from a long smear on the pane nearest her. Pressed against the bloody smear was an arm in a leather jacket, and above it, the aquiline profile of Breaker was silhouetted against the afternoon sky. Even against the brightness, he looked pale, his eyes squeezed shut. He must not have heard her scream.

She ran to the door and then stopped. Karol had warned her, Breaker was a criminal, and nothing Breaker had said had contradicted that. Certainly fleeing the scene of a crime, hiding from someone hired by the police, and now turning up on her patio bleeding from a wound in the shoulder didn't inspire a great deal of trust. Her hand fluttered over the door handle and then pulled her cell phone from her pocket.

She'd left Karol's card in the kitchen. In the doorway between the kitchen and living room, she hesitated. Breaker had turned and was staring in at her now, not talking, just watching her with those dark brown eyes. He's a criminal, Valerie told herself, a wanted man.

But for what? Karol hadn't told her. Wouldn't it be easy to say, "he's a bank robber," or "he's a con artist," or even, "he's a murderer"? If he were really dangerous, he'd had plenty of opportunity to attack her when they were alone in the boat, or on the beach after landing. But he'd just wanted to get away from her.

His right hand was still inside his jacket, holding the wound in his side. From his left shoulder, through the jacket, the shaft of an arrow protruded. That was where the blood on her window had come from.

Who hunts criminals with a bow and arrow? She glanced once more at Karol's business card. *Professionals.* The empty quiver on Anton's back.

Her mother had called during the divorce. "I hope you'll find someone who deserves you," she'd said. Mom always thought Val was attracted to the wrong kind of men. Moms always thought that, of course. She would flip out right now if she knew Val was standing in her living room actually entertaining the idea of letting an injured possible-criminal into her home. "Haven't you learned anything?" she'd shriek.

If he'd asked for help, if he'd begged or pleaded, perversely, she might have called Karol right then. But he just stood there silently, and she knew that if she didn't let him in, he would be over the side of the deck and into the woods before she'd finished dialing. And it was that consideration for her, the fact that he would accept her decision, that led her to the patio door, to unlatch it and pull it open. "Come on," she said. "If you're on the run, you need to get cleaned up."

He didn't move right away. Then he nodded, a curt acknowledgment, and stumbled into the living room.

She closed the door and latched it again. He watched her, swaying where he was standing, and then he crumpled to the floor.

Blood spread across the soft white rug. "Oh, God," Valerie said. For it to be spreading so quickly was not good. The arrow must have hit an artery. First aid, she'd seen the first aid kit in the kitchen, one of the first things she'd looked for when she arrived. She hurried to get it, opening it as she returned and pulling out the roll of gauze and medicated pads. Get pressure on the wound first, then bind it up.

But there's going to have to be a hospital involved, she thought. She didn't have the training to deal with a punctured artery. She knelt beside him and grasped the shaft of the arrow, the urgency of the task allowing her to ignore the smell and sight of blood, for the moment.

"No," Breaker growled.

Valerie started. "You're awake? I need to get the jacket off."

He nodded. "Pull it out."

"But—"

"Pull it out!" He seemed to be forcing the words past an obstruction in his throat.

"All right," she said. "It's gonna hurt. Let me get you something to bite down on."

His face was almost grey now. "Pocket," he gasped, inclining his head to the right.

She reached into the right-hand pocket of his jacket and found a leathery cylinder, a rolled-up piece of hide that had plenty of toothmarks on it. He opened his mouth and let her put it between his teeth, chewing down and closing his eyes.

Valerie grasped the shaft of the arrow and set her other hand against his shoulder. She had no idea how to get an arrow out of a wound, so she started working it from side to side, pulling as she did. Breaker moaned, his body twitching; even through the jacket she could feel the knotted muscle in his shoulder. "Hang on," she said. It felt like the arrow was caught on something, as though the tip were barbed. She pulled harder, eliciting a loud groan from Breaker, but still the arrow wouldn't come.

"Moon," he growled around the hide.

"Uh-huh." She continued to work at the arrow, with no success.

"Call the moon," he said, distinctly.

He's hallucinating, she thought. "Here, moon. C'mere, moon," she murmured, focused more on why the stubborn arrow refused to budge.

"Ask. The. Moon. For. Help." Each word was an effort for him.

"Stop talking," she snapped. "All right, all right." Out the patio window, the sky was a clear blue. She had no idea where the moon was. "O Moon," she said.

"Call her…mother."

It took her a moment to realize that he'd meant "call the moon your mother" and not "call the moon's mother." She sighed. If it would help him relax, she'd recite whatever he wanted. She took hold of the arrow. "O Moon, my mother, help me get this arrow out. Please."

A small static electricity shock snapped through Valerie's fingertips. She jerked back in surprise and the arrow came with her, cleanly and easily like a fish through water.

Breaker sank back onto the carpet, the small rolled hide falling from his mouth. She only spared a moment to stare at the arrow before tossing it aside, because when the jacket fell open, she could see blood spurting from the shoulder. Femoral artery, was that it? Didn't matter, just get pressure on it. She pressed a gauze pad to the neat circular wound, noting a small rash around it. Nothing as extensive as the wound in his side, which was much worse than she remembered it being, and still had the broken-off shaft sunk into it.

Blood soaked the pad quickly. She pressed down harder, reaching for another pad from the first aid kit. Breaker wasn't reacting to anything now, while his life kept pulsing wetly against her hand. She gritted her teeth, swapping the clean pad for the soaked and bloody one. The first aid kit had instructions on it, about getting a bandage around the limb to staunch the flow of blood, but she couldn't read them from where she was. There were only two more pads within reach, so if the bleeding didn't go down soon, she would have to improvise.

Of course, if the bleeding didn't go down soon, he would die. How fast did arteries heal? Would they start to repair themselves in five minutes? She'd never been near the site of a major injury. Even the time she'd broken her arm, it hadn't been bleeding, just painful and swollen. Plus, she'd been nine at the time.

The new pad was soaked through almost as fast as the last one. She tried to pull it away, but it was sticky and so she just put the third pad on top of it, pressing down as hard as she could. Her own breathing sounded loud as a hurricane in her ears, the only sound she could hear. She couldn't tell whether Breaker was still breathing, though his heart was definitely beating.

More weakly, though. She pressed harder, trying to re-situate her fingers without losing any pressure, but she couldn't find the strong pulses she'd felt before. Was it healing or was he dying? Valerie closed her eyes and held her hands against his bare shoulder, wishing there were more she could do as his life leaked out through her fingers.

A ridiculous notion came to her. "Oh, Moon," she said under her breath, "help me make him well."

She opened her eyes and waited, but she felt no answering shock in her fingertips, no change in the weakening pulses beneath them. The new pad didn't seem to be getting soaked as quickly. Was that only her imagination? The smell of blood was making her a little nauseous, but she leaned forward anyway.

She could still see some white threads in the gauze, while the pad below was a sodden mass of maroon. So the bleeding was slowing. And now that she moved closer, she could see the flutter in Breaker's chest that indicated breathing.

She exhaled, slowly. Carefully, she reached for the roll of tape and bound the dressing to his shoulder, keeping the gauze as tight to the wound as she could manage. When she'd finished, the tape was bloody with her fingerprints and his dark shoulder showed smears and patches of blood all over it, but at least he was breathing, demonstrably alive.

The dressing gave her a sense of accomplishment. She sat back on her heels, not even nauseous from the smell of blood any more. She did want to wash her hands, very much, but she forced herself to wait to see that the dressing would hold, and in the meantime found her gaze traveling along the well-defined muscles in his arm, the tight curves of his stomach visible even through the fine layer of black hair. The other arrow, broken, was still stuck in his left side, his rash now flame-red around it.

Well, she thought, he's unconscious now. No time like the present. She lay one hand on his side, grasping the broken shaft in the other. His skin was fluttering with life, but chill to the touch. Again, she tried working the arrow to pull it out, and again, it felt as though barbs were catching on it. This time, she looked at the arrow she'd discarded. The tip was smooth and shiny, not even textured, let alone barbed.

If this arrow were the same, that didn't make any sense. Unless it had lodged in bone, but there was no bone where this one had landed. She moved her hand, placing it on his stomach. Only to brace herself, she said, even though her pulse quickened and she felt a sharp rush at the touch. Even when she pulled harder, wincing in sympathy, the arrow remained stuck in him.

Valerie glanced out the patio door to the sky beyond. "O Mother Moon," she said softly. "Help me remove this arrow, please."

Her fingers tingled. The wooden shaft slid out of Breaker's side easily and fell into her hand.

Chapter 5

She held up the broken arrow to the sunlight. The head of this one was silver, as smooth and glossy as the other. Now that she was looking close up, she could see a small circle inscribed around its tip with an inscription below it in some Slavic language she couldn't decipher. She was about to set it down when she noticed the wooden shaft sparkling in the light. Curious, she brought it closer and saw silver filaments, as narrow as a human hair, running lengthwise in the wood grain along the shaft.

That was a lot of silver to put into an arrow, considering an arrow was usually shot once and then lost. She weighed the broken shaft and then picked up the whole one. It too had a circle around the tip with the same inscription below it, and the silver filaments ran the length of the arrow, to the pure white feathers at the end.

She took them both into the kitchen where she washed her hands in the sink, scrubbing long after the last trace of blood had washed down the drain, thinking about Breaker and Karol and the arrows while the warm water ran over her fingers. Karol's card lay on the counter, stark white against the brown tile, the word *Professionals* jumping out from the background. Breaker lay in her living room, a good amount of his blood on her rug. She was going to have to wait 'til he woke up, because she wasn't strong enough to move him to a bed without help. And the arrows, the ones that Anton and presumably Karol had been shooting, that Breaker was unable to remove, that she was unable to remove until she'd said some nonsense prayer to the moon…

The arrows lay on the counter. By rights, the tips should be slick with blood, but only the wooden shafts bore any trace of red. The silver tips gleamed brightly in the sun from the window over the sink. The whole moon business could have been merely psychological, but there was still something unsettling about the arrows themselves.

She left them on the sink while she went in search of an old towel or blanket. She found a stack of old flannel sheets in the bottom of a linen closet and decided they would have to do. Breaker was still out, and didn't wake when she pulled the sheets over him. She left a bottle of water at his side in case he woke while she was gone.

She didn't like leaving him alone, but she wanted to pick up some better food, some bandages, and a steam cleaner for the carpet. And she wanted to ask some people some questions. The only person she knew who definitely knew both Anton and Breaker was Leon, and since she needed supplies anyway, that was a good place to start.

Leon's store was moderately busy when she entered. Valerie walked around, filling her basket with anti-bacterial ointment and two boxes of sterile pads, canned chicken soup and loaves of bread, whole chicken breasts and steaks. Only after she'd put the steaks in the basket did she look down bemusedly and think, am I planning a steak dinner? Breaker seemed like a very steak-and-potatoes guy. Sure, like he's going to stick around for dinner. He'll either be gone when I get back, or ready for a trip to the hospital. But she added some vegetables and potatoes anyway, and by the time she walked up to Leon, there were only a few other people in the store, browsing near the back.

He didn't have steam cleaners, but he gave her directions to Geneseo, forty-five minutes away, where he said the Long's Drugs should have one for rent. "Got your appetite up," he said, ringing up the items. "Good day hiking?"

"No," she said automatically, and then suppressed the impulse to tell the truth. "I mean, not a full day. Had to stop just after noon. Scratched up my leg." She indicated the ointment.

He glanced at the pads. "Must be some scratch."

"Oh, those are just restocking Martin's first aid kit," she said lightly. "I went looking for the ointment and saw he let a few things get low."

"That's Martin." He laughed. "If I didn't put firewood aside for him every October, he'd freeze his ass off in November. Pardon my French."

She chuckled. "You don't have to tell me. I work for him."

He winked. "Bet that means you do a lot of his work for him."

"Well, I wouldn't put it exactly that way..." But she grinned in such a way as to tell him she would. "Say, I meant to ask...that man who was in here last night?"

His face darkened. "What about 'im?"

"I mean, the man who was buying groceries when I came in. You were talking about kayaks?"

"Oh." He smiled. "Anton. Right. What about him?"

"Well." Her heart beat faster. "I do like getting off on my own, but I was getting a little lonely today. Just wondering...is he single? Does he live around here?"

She'd hoped that Leon's sympathy from the previous evening would translate into helpful information, and she wasn't disappointed. "I've never seen him with a woman," Leon said, rubbing his beard. "Sure, he's actually renting a place about half a mile down from where Martin's is. I can't give you the number, but I'm sure he wouldn't mind if you stopped by." As he scribbled an address on a scrap of paper, he said, "He's one of the better-looking guys around here. Most of 'em look like me."

Valerie took the paper and laughed. "If I hadn't seen the wedding ring on your finger, I might be asking you to share one of these steaks."

Leon laughed heartily. "I tell you what, if you want to invite Annie and me by one evening, we wouldn't say no. Wouldn't mind if Anton were there, either. He's a little strange, but interesting."

She nodded, then tilted her head. "Strange, like how?"

"Oh, nothing bad," he said. "But he eats a lot of meat. I mean, a lot. Hadda change my weekly order 'cause of him. I asked if he had dogs, but he said no, he just likes his steaks. So I guess he just hunts for trophies."

"Oh, he's a hunter."

Leon nodded. "That turn you off?" Valerie shook her head. "There's some asshole hunters for sure, but he's a bow hunter. Those guys, I respect. You gotta get real close to the prey and gotta have a steady hand. It's a lot more dangerous than just sittin' in a blind and shooting a rifle at a hundred feet."

"I bet." Valerie mentally urged the woman meandering toward them to stop and look at something, not to come directly to the counter. "So he hunts deer?"

"That's about all you can hunt up here. But they ain't in season for a month yet, so I dunno. Maybe he just spends six months taking target practice." He laughed.

"He's been renting here that long?"

"Oh, not the whole time." Leon frowned slightly. "Lessee, it was March he first came in here. No, it was April, I remember, 'cause we had nice weather and that was just after that girl..."

He didn't have to finish. Valerie saw the story in his hasty silence. "There was an accident?"

"There's been two," a woman's voice said behind her. The other shopper set her basket down on the counter. "But they were no accidents. Wolfs got 'em."

Leon had turned back to his register. "Forty-three fifteen, Valerie."

She handed him her debit card and turned back to the woman. "Wolves?"

"Yep." The woman had loosely curled blond hair with streaks of silver in it, pinned back over her ears. She wasn't wearing any makeup, nor, Valerie thought, any women's clothing: her flannel shirt looked like it had come from the same rack as Leon's, and her patched pants had clearly come from an army surplus store, if not from a thrift shop behind an army surplus store. "Young lady in April, found her down just off the road." She clutched her throat, staring at Valerie. "Throat torn out."

"Willie," Leon said, "Valerie don't need to hear all that. It's safe now." He handed back her card and waited while she signed the slip. "Safer than New York City."

"You keep to the roads and you'll be safe," Willie said. "The other one was fifteen. Poor little kid. Wandered away from the campground." She clutched her throat again. "Didn't find her 'til a week later."

Leon pulled Willie's basket toward him. "Don't you listen to her," he told Valerie, starting to ring up the items. "Some folks don't like it bein' so peaceful here, so they dwell on accidents. Makes their lives excitin'."

"Warn't no accidents," Willie said. "Wolfs always been good 'round here. Somethin' drove 'em bad this year. Damn shame. Happens, though."

"Maybe they were just hungry." Valerie hefted her bag of food.

Willie laughed, a screechy, unnerving sound. "How can they go hungry when they can come to Leon's? Eh, Leon? Eh?"

"You take care of those scratches, miss," Leon said to Valerie. "And tell Anton I said to take good care of ya."

Valerie checked the address, driving back. She wanted to check out the house, but she was worried she'd find Karol there and that he would ask more awkward questions. Besides, the meat needed to go in the fridge. And she wanted to check on Breaker.

He was still out on the living room floor. She checked the bandages. Though the crusting over was disgusting, at least it was better than a pulsing arterial wound. And the rash wasn't as bad as she'd remembered it being. The swelling around his side had gone down, and the angry line under his collarbone was a mere discoloration. The color had returned to his face, and he seemed altogether more peaceful.

She drew the blanket back over him, and then drew the curtains across the patio doors. Should have done that to begin with. Then she sat on the sofa and stared at the wounded man on her floor, then got up and walked to the kitchen, then came back to the living room.

She had to go; she didn't feel like sitting around waiting for Breaker to wake up, unable to focus on anything else. Just a short trip to get a steam cleaner, she told herself, and then right back here. But when she got into her car and set out, she turned right and drove half a mile, the address Leon had given her burning in her head.

Not going to break any laws, she told herself. Just going to look around, see if I can find out anything more about him. And if Karol and his truck are anywhere around, well, I'll just drive on.

Even to herself, the rationale seemed thin. If she'd brought his wallet, she realized, she would be able to claim she'd found it and was trying to give it back. But of course, that would lead to other questions about where she'd found it. She shook her head. It was hard to stick to the truth when the truth was so slippery. Making it especially hard was that she didn't know what she expected to find. There was just a nagging sense of curiosity about the mysterious Anton and his brother, a need to find out whether helping Breaker was the right thing to do or a terrible mistake.

The house Anton had been renting sat back a hundred feet from the road, a neatly-kept cabin surrounded by trees. The black truck was nowhere to be seen, so she parked a little ways down the lane and walked up, listening to the air around her. Birds sang, squirrels made their merry way through the trees, but she heard no cars save for the occasional engine sound on the distant road, no other noise of people.

The enclosed porch looked ridiculously normal: a weathered plastic lounge chair in one corner, a doormat, a small sign for the rental agency. "Hello?" she called.

No answer came. She walked around the house, looking at the windows at eye level. There was nothing in the cabin that looked extraordinary or odd; it was as neat inside as outside, tidy and vacuumed as if it were ready for rental. An easy chair sat facing a hi-def TV; an immaculate kitchen gleamed in the sunlight; a bed waited, neatly made, for its owner to return. If not for the folded clothes on the dresser near the bed, and a single empty glass on a side table by the TV chair, she would think Anton had packed up to leave.

The back door was shut firmly. She resisted the urge to try it to see whether it was locked. When she came around the far side of the house, though, she came across a storm cellar, and the window leading into the basement was cracked open. Valerie looked around again, but still heard nobody in the area. She knelt and peered through the opening.

At last, a room that looked lived-in. On the table just below the window, she saw a curious arrangement of animal teeth and small rocks, arrayed in a circle. To one side of the table, small glass jars sat, but she couldn't see the contents. A wooden chair had been pushed back from the table, and behind it…Valerie strained to see in the dim light. It looked like a small field of wheat. Fake, it had to be. You couldn't grow wheat indoors. But the way it moved in the shadows, swaying slightly, looked unnervingly real. Together with the animal teeth, it looked like the study of some twisted witch doctor from a horror film.

She stood, brushing the knees of her pants clean. For a moment, she stared at the storm cellar doors. Of course, they would be locked, but if they weren't…if she just looked around, nobody would know. Curiosity burned at her.

"I'll look," she said aloud, and bent to the storm cellar. The door came up an inch, and then a latch rattled inside, stopping her progress.

She walked around to the front, oddly disappointed. One last look at the house yielded no further insights, so she strolled along the lane, lost in thought until she came in sight of her car. She stopped short. A black pickup truck was parked behind it, and leaning against the passenger side door of her car, in his immaculate white suit, was Karol Vojacek.

Chapter 6

He raised a hand to her as she drew nearer. "Hello, Miss Creighton," he said. "I spotted your car sitting here and worried you might have become lost."

She shook her head. "I was just...Leon at the grocery store gave me the address..."

"If you wanted to reach Anton, you had but to call the number I left."

She didn't want to walk closer, but she couldn't come up with a good reason not to. Karol's ice-blue eyes glinted in the sun. Her mind raced. "I remembered I saw Anton at Leon's," she said. "I wanted to see if I could find him."

"Mm." He stroked his chin with long fingers. His face, where the sun hit it, was as luminous as if it were carved from soapstone.

"And." She lowered her voice and her eyes. "To tell the truth, after talking to you, I didn't feel very safe in my own house. Leon didn't know where you're staying, and I didn't want to bother you for that."

She still had a little charm left, it seemed. His face broke into a smile. "Well, I am sorry to have frightened you," he said. "I believe it is best to be fully informed and a little frightened than to feel safe through ignorance."

"I don't blame you," she said. "But the thought of that criminal, running around the woods..."

He frowned, slightly. Perhaps she was laying it on a little thick. "Yes," he said. "Unfortunately, I have had no more success in finding him. However, if you like, I will accompany you back to your house. With the door locked, you will be perfectly safe, I am sure. A charming and intelligent young woman such as yourself has little to—"

His hand had touched her elbow, a prelude, she supposed, to walking her back to her car, but when his fingers brushed the material of her shirt, a small crackle of static electricity snapped between them. He stopped talking and stared, eyes searching hers.

"Looks like we made sparks," she said, as lightly as she could.

"Indeed." His eyes slid to the side, toward something in the sky she couldn't see, and then back to her. "Miss Creighton, would you care to join me for a cup of tea? Or coffee, if you prefer the American version."

"It's Mrs. Creighton," she said.

"I do apologize. Is Mr. Creighton at the house?"

"No, I'm...he's not here. It just sounds strange, 'Miss Creighton.'" She rubbed her elbow, unable to take her eyes from his face. "I'll be glad to join you for tea. Would you mind going up to Geneseo? I need to run an errand there, anyway."

It was better than having him follow her back to the house, she told herself, getting into her car. So why did she now feel a strange eagerness to get closer to him? It was the spark, the connection between them. His eyes had lit up when he'd felt that, and the smooth mask she was used to seeing had fallen away. There was something real behind that mask.

Following him down the lane, she looked to the side, where he'd looked, but saw nothing there but trees. He led her along the lakeside road to a minor highway, a forty-five minute drive to Geneseo, where he stopped at a Starbucks. She almost laughed, the location so normal after all the strangeness that had happened over the last day that again, as she had that afternoon, she had the impression that it might all be a dream. Surely she couldn't be sitting in a Starbucks, sipping a grande non-fat cappuccino, after seeing one man die and saving another from bleeding to death. And yet she was here, the milk and coffee just on the right side of scalding, and so close to her that she could smell the dry, earthy smell that seemed at odds with his immaculate white suit was Karol Vojacek.

"I grew up a farmer," he said, as if aware of the earthy smell, "back in the old country. I have always loved the land, and all natural things that grow from it." He held up one hand, long white fingers immaculately groomed, and laughed. "I have not farmed in some time now. But I have not lost my love for the land. The land here is not rich, as it is in the old country, but it is no less healthy and beautiful for all that. And the people here love their land as we did. You can see it."

She looked around the coffee shop and nodded, though all she really saw was a lot of men in business casual dress. One man, in the corner, wore a denim shirt and jeans, scuffed and dirty, but she couldn't really picture him as a farmer while he was sipping from a Starbucks cup. "So you want to live here?"

"Oh, no." He laughed, looking out the front window at the quiet street and the hills beyond. "I go wherever the land is threatened."

"You're a professional," she said.

His eyes returned to her. "Just so." He smiled.

"Professional...what?" Her cappuccino tasted the same as the one she got every morning in the city. The familiar ritual gave her more confidence. "Lawyer? Bounty hunter?"

"Whatever is necessary."

His hair glowed in the sunlight. Silver it might be, but it wasn't thinning, not by any stretch of the imagination, the foremost locks shadowing his forehead. With half his face in sun and half in shadow, he looked like a marble statue in a museum, and she realized that if it weren't for his hair, she would have no idea how old he was. His ice-blue eyes watched her, bright and undisturbed by the sun pouring across them. She set her cup down. "I didn't know there was a land fight here. What is necessary?"

He set down his cup, giving her a whiff of the strong black tea it contained, and looked thoughtfully at her. "The fight is subtle. It is a poison that is infecting the land so slowly that the people may not even be aware of it."

Valerie frowned. Hadn't he said the police had called him? "You mean like chemical waste?"

"Something like that." His nose wrinkled as if he'd caught whiff of a bad smell, and his eyebrows lowered as he leaned in toward her. "I am particularly sensitive to certain kinds of...pollution." He seemed about to say more, but stopped to pick up his cup of tea and drink from it, and that broke his momentum. The silver ring on his middle left finger gleamed in the sunlight.

He leaned back in his chair, the frown still on his face. He wasn't looking at Valerie at all. "Like a skin condition?" she said, at length.

He turned slowly to her. "Excuse me?"

"You said you're sensitive…" She trailed off. He had leaned forward at her words and nodded.

"Not a skin condition. I mean I am particularly easily upset. My father was killed by…waste, as you say."

Valerie felt an echo of years-ago pain. "I'm so sorry," she said. "I lost my father to cancer too."

"Yes," he said. "You understand. It is a cancer. It is a wrongness that eats at the earth. It may sit quietly for years, centuries even, but eventually the wrongness will spread and corrupt the surrounding area."

He had begun to flush around his cheekbones, spots of red in his otherwise pale face. Valerie wrapped her fingers around the cup. "Centuries," she echoed. "I didn't know they had factories that long ago."

"Waste," he said darkly, "can be produced in many different ways." He sighed. "I'm sorry. I am worried about my brother."

Guilt flared up in Valerie. "He's probably working hard."

He gave her a curious look. "I expected to find him at home. As did you, I suppose."

"Shouldn't you be waiting for him there?"

He smiled, then. "He will not be waiting for me. If he is indeed working, as you suggest, or if he has fallen victim to…well, then it will make no difference if I am there or here. And I would very much prefer to be here."

She felt a warm flush, lifting her cappuccino to hide her sudden nervousness. "I appreciate you taking the time."

"It is my pleasure."

They sat in silence, listening to the murmur of conversation around them. People nearby were talking about the local bank, about the storm expected the following day, about the low number of tourists. Valerie said, impulsively, "I had heard there were wolf attacks. Earlier in the season. Have you seen any wolves around?"

She hadn't expected his expression to darken again, as it had when he was talking about the chemical waste. "I have not," he said.

"I thought…I thought you might be here to help control the wolves."

He nodded, his body tensing as though he'd spotted a wolf right there in the coffee shop. "That we are, Mrs. Creighton."

"Val," she said. "But aren't wolves part of nature? I mean," she allowed herself a small chuckle, "you're the expert, but I've seen documentaries and I know there are places where they're a nuisance, but still…"

He reached out very deliberately and touched her hand. There was no spark, but she felt a small tingle. "Wolves, yes," he said, lowering his voice. "But these are not natural wolves."

His fingers were warm. The smell of tea filled her head, drowning out her cappuccino. "Not natural? Like...genetically modified?"

His low chuckle didn't lighten his expression. "Just so. Val, do you believe in spirits?"

He was earnest and serious, and the only reason she didn't excuse herself right there and then was the wash of relief at figuring out just what kind of kook he was. Creepiness wasn't as frightening when she could put a name to it, like "new age pagan spiritualist." The best thing to do with these guys was just agree with whatever they said and then make an excuse to leave at the first opportunity. "Well," she said, as though thinking about it, "sometimes I kind of sense that my dad is near. You know?"

"Mm. The dead often linger in our memories, remaining almost tangibly real. I understand what you mean. But I am talking about real spirits. I am talking about the supernatural."

That was a little odd, Valerie had to confess. Usually the new age folks ate up the dead father bit. She'd even gotten subjected to a ouija board session once. The coffee shop still comforted her with its bland normality, though. Behind the counter, the baristas were joking with each other in easy camaraderie; at the corner table, one of the two young women in business casual clothes was pointing to the sky outside. "The supernatural," she said.

"You are thinking that I am crazy," he said. "But I assure you that I am very sane."

"Oh, of course." She gulped down her cappuccino, trying to finish it. "I know, 'there are more things on Heaven and Earth, Horatio,' and all that. I'm totally behind that."

"Look." He pulled the teabag out of his cup and rested it on the plastic lid. Covering it with one hand, he closed his eyes. When he pulled his hand away, she saw small green shoots sticking out of the teabag, with tiny curled leaves at the end.

"I am a guardian of fields and cultivated plants," he said. "I have a certain...rapport with them."

Val stared at the small shoots in the teabag, and then shook her head. There were no seeds in tea, she was pretty sure, so it wasn't like it even made sense that he was making something sprout. He probably just kept those little green shoots around to create the illusion that he could, and he hadn't even been that good at the sleight-of-hand. He'd just covered the teabag while he poked the fake shoots into it. So he was a new age pagan after all, just a fairly specifically focused one. With a flair for amateur drama. "That's great." She nodded, pretending to study the small plant. "That's really great."

He studied her. "But just as there are benevolent spirits, there are also abominations."

She checked to see whether anyone was close enough to hear them, but the two young women were still going on about the weather, and the farmer-looking guy had left fifteen minutes ago. "And these wolves..."

He brought the tea to his lips and sipped it. "I believe you would call them werewolves."

The word startled a laugh out of her. She tried to turn it into a cough, but his eyes narrowed in disapproval. Great. The one thing these guys hated was when you mocked their beliefs. "Sorry," she said. "It's just...I've seen too many movies."

"Your movies make light of the threat," he said.

She frowned. "I'm not sure what movies you've seen. They always seem pretty scary to me."

"To individuals," he said. "The true threat runs much deeper. They befoul the land with their very nature. Their perverse magic saps the strength of the surrounding wilderness. Could you but hear the plants, you would hear their cries for help every time the moon is full and the waste gathers strength."

Valerie looked down at the teabag again, the small green plant. "I'm sure it's horrible." She didn't know what else to say. She wished for the scream of a tornado, wished a fire would break out, wished a car would smash into the front of the coffee shop. It had been a long time since she'd wanted to get out of a conversation this badly. The blind date, a couple months before she'd met Steven, with the lawyer who wouldn't shut up about the "'86 Mets" who had won something or another. That name, along with someone named "Mookie," was now lodged in her memory next to the uncomfortable feeling that there was no way for her to politely extricate herself from the situation, which was probably why she was remembering it now.

Karol was still talking. "The people around here become complacent. Just as the industrial waste you know of seeps into the ground and rests there, unnoticed, so does this waste ingratiate itself, masquerading as part of the community."

The word "community" gave her an in. "We have people like that in our neighborhood. They just live there, sometimes they take things, they don't give anything back. It's really frustrating."

"Yes. Just so. There are rules." He slapped the table with his open palm. "Those who do not abide by the rules set down by nature are an affront, a cancer."

She hated when people abused the term 'cancer.' Cancer was a disease, not a slacker who didn't care enough about his neighbors to keep his yard clear. But the number one rule of living in the city, if you wanted to get along with people, was 'don't screw with crazy.' "Sure," she said. "I feel the same way."

"Good." He smiled, leaning back as though he'd accomplished something.

She pushed the empty paper cup around the table. "So this criminal you're looking for...he's a..."

He leaned in toward her. "One of the worst. He's responsible for the killings."

The smell of earth felt oppressive now, like mud tracked in when Steven had been out back in his tool shed and come in from the rain. She felt she had to warn Breaker now that this lunatic had developed a fixation on him. Although, she reflected, he probably already knew that, considering he'd been shot twice with arrows. Arrows that wouldn't come out of him easily. That had been tipped and laced with silver.

She shook that thought off. Imagination, that's all it was. "I will certainly call you if I see him," she said, and as if on cue, her cell phone chirped. "Oh, I haven't had good reception anywhere since I got to the cabin." She flipped it open and saw a text message from Martin: *Enjoying the lake?*

Since when did he check up on her on vacation? Since her divorce, of course. Still, maybe what he really meant was: *are you trashing my house?* She snapped the phone shut. "Something wrong?" Karol asked.

It would be convenient to lie, but she couldn't bring herself to lie completely. "Maybe," she said. "I do need to run that errand before it gets too late."

"Of course," he said, and stood with her, extending a hand. "I do so much appreciate you allowing me to take up your time."

"Oh, no, thank you for explaining your work." His hand was warm and firm. "I understand the importance of it much better now."

"Excellent. It has truly been a pleasure making your acquaintance, Val. Please, allow me." He picked up her empty cup in addition to his own.

He walked behind her out to their cars. As she was getting in, he held up a hand and said, "One more thing. The moon is full tomorrow night. Best to stay indoors, no matter what."

"Of course." She paused, standing just inside her door, the sun warm on her back. "Because of the werewolves."

There was nobody on the sidewalk to hear them, but Karol looked around to make sure before answering. "I would not warn you did I not think the warning necessary."

What did that mean? she wondered, driving over to the drugstore to get the steam cleaner. She was still thinking about that, driving home with the sunset in her rear view mirror. Did he know, had he guessed, that she'd helped Breaker? That shock, that tingle she'd felt when she touched him,

(the same as when she'd called the moon)

what did that mean?

Static electricity, nothing more significant than that. But clearly he'd been making pointed remarks about her going out during the full moon. Maybe...maybe he had an elaborate listening device. He might have heard her inside her home. Those crazy types, especially the ones that fancied themselves vigilantes, often got military-grade spy equipment from barely-legal websites. Maybe it was worth a call to the police station at Lake Wahya, just to see if they really had called him in for help.

Breaker seemed to think they had, but his behavior hadn't been much more stable. Though honestly, if Anton had been anywhere near as off as his brother, she couldn't blame Breaker for running from the corpse. Anton had probably stabbed him with the arrow, after all, thinking he was doing the right thing, eliminating a cancer, however they wanted to put it.

Val felt the unreality of the situation creep over her again. The thought of the two brothers roaming around the lake, stalking Breaker and maybe others, was distinctly unsettling. Maybe if she left the lake, Breaker would want to come with her. Get out of the area, let Karol hunt around fruitlessly for a while. She could find a place near a bigger lake, a larger town, where it'd be easier for them to be anonymous.

And then what? She jerked herself back to reality. He certainly hadn't shown much interest in her company; did she think he'd hop in a car with her and take off for a week? And just what was she thinking they would *do* for a week? What, Val, just because you're finally legally free to mess around, you think a guy half your age (well, she allowed, probably not that young) will just hop in the car (or bed) with you? And surely, surely, there are more eligible candidates for a post-divorce fling than a shady young man being hunted by two—er, one mercenary?

Even if you did get to rest your hand on his stomach. Even if it has been six? seven? months since you touched a man's stomach (and that was just to show Steven how much weight he'd put on). Even if your fingers sparked, and you know it's just static electricity. Even if, even if, even if.

She sighed and shook her head, switching on her headlights as she turned the car back onto the lakeside road. She could fantasize all she wanted. What would happen is she'd get back, she'd tell Breaker that he had to go to the hospital, he'd refuse, she'd tell him she was going to head somewhere else for a week, and he'd look at her with those dark brown eyes and shrug and say, "Probably a good choice."

Movement caught her eye at the side of the road. She slowed, then stopped as a deer poked its head cautiously out into the road. It trotted across, giving her nervous glances as it did. She started rolling forward again, only to slam her foot on the brake as a second deer leapt out from the shadows, passing within a foot of her bumper and darting into the woods on the other side.

Heart pounding, she sat in the car until she saw headlights behind her and had to start moving. Christ, she thought, crazy people and wolf attacks weren't enough. Now the deer are after me too.

She was so preoccupied that she missed the turn to Martin's cabin at first. There was plenty of light from the moon, which looked full to her despite what Karol had said about the full moon being tomorrow; she'd just rolled past the street without thinking. She turned back and drove up the dirt lane, got out, and was halfway to the cabin before the feeling of being watched came over her like a powerful wave.

She turned to one side, then the other, and saw nothing, heard nothing but the crickets and the scurrying of mice here and there. You're still spooked from the deer, she told herself, and took another couple steps. But the feeling wouldn't go away. She glanced up at the moon. It should be giving enough light for her to see anything nearby. Feeling a bit silly, she murmured under her breath, "Mother Moon, show me whatever is watching me."

To her right, not ten feet away, something gleamed in the darkness. She turned and saw two points of light, silver reflections of the moon, staring at her. Slowly, a shape stepped out of the shadows, a large, low animal shape whose silhouette was somehow blacker than the shadows. It reminded her of her German Shepherd, only much larger, much quieter, and much more self-assured than Benjy had ever been. She had no trouble identifying it as a wolf. Had she not been able to see its head, she might have thought it was a small pony.

It was standing with its right side toward her, head turned to watch her, as though it had been about to walk down to the road when she had interrupted it. She held her breath, her memory coming up with nothing helpful about what to do when you're standing ten feet away from a wild animal that could rip your throat out as soon as look at you. Don't run, she told herself, or it'll see you as prey (like Benjy used to chase her around the house, only not like that at all). Just stand still. If it attacks, then run to the car. She gripped the keys in her pocket and it occurred to her that she could use them as weapons, as if she were being mugged in the city, something she had read about but never actually experienced.

The wolf turned to face her, and that was the first time she noticed that it was limping, favoring its left leg. A patch of white glowed around the left shoulder, in the light of the moon, as if...as if...it had been bandaged.

Heart hammering in her chest, Valerie held her breath. The wolf's eyes still glowed with the moon, watching her intelligently. Slowly, it turned its head and grasped the bandage in long, pointed teeth. It pulled, and the white fabric came away with a soft tearing sound. Holding the bandage in its teeth, the wolf stepped forward.

Valerie jumped back. The wolf limped to within a foot of the path, moving slowly, and set the bandage down. It raised its head, and then— and this was impossible—it bowed. And then it was gone.

Her knees almost didn't make it to the front door. She collapsed against it, fumbling for the key. That was impossible. She would walk in, and Breaker would be lying there on the floor. Maybe he would be awake, and he would give her one of those cynical looks she had already come to expect. Or a smile, in gratitude, a fleeting thing. Or he would still be unconscious; after all, he'd lost a lot of blood.

The door gave way. She fell inside, slammed it behind her, and leaned against the wall, breathing hard. Okay, Val, collect yourself. You're okay. You're okay. You can handle this. Just go and see Breaker, and you'll know. You'll know that wasn't...what Karol said it was.

But she knew before she even entered the living room what she would really see when she flicked the light switch: the enormous red stain on the floor, the glass empty of the water she'd left and set neatly on the coffee table, and nothing else. Breaker was gone.

Chapter 7

Of course he's gone. He turned into a wolf and said thank you and trotted off into the forest, to hunt deer or rabbits or

(little girls)

whatever it is that wolves hunt.

She brought herself up sharply. All you have is circumstantial evidence, she reminded herself. A wolf who didn't attack you, who was bandaged. It probably...it probably was being treated at a center near here, and was just released. And it was conditioned not to attack humans. Because it'd been under treatment for so long.

The construction of this elaborate explanation felt shaky even as she were trying to shore it up with her faith. Martin had to have a liquor cabinet somewhere, dammit. She found it, finally, in the living room just below the bookcase. He had a nice twelve-year-old scotch, which she poured into a tumbler and downed. The rich fire of the alcohol seared away the shakiness, grounding her back in reality.

Then she felt strong enough to go to the car to get the cleaner, but the woods seemed to be watching her, even though the strong feeling was gone. She read the steamer instructions through three times before realizing she hadn't absorbed even one word of them. Probably it was hunger. She hadn't eaten since coming back from the canoeing at noon, eating that sandwich out on the patio.

She went to the kitchen to fix herself something to eat for dinner, because she had to do something normal, but none of the instant meals looked appetizing. Something normal, she thought. Chicken noodle soup, or a thick stew. It would be good to talk to Leon, too. She could ask about the police, about a wildlife treatment center nearby. And it would be good to get her away from this house, where the silence felt like a living thing crouched out on the patio, waiting for the right moment to pounce.

Karol's card lay on the kitchen counter. She hesitated, then grabbed it and stuffed it in her pocket. The other thing she didn't want to face about the cliff she was refusing to look over was that on the other side, Karol was not only sane, he was perhaps the most important person she'd met.

The door to Leon's grocery was locked when she got there, but Leon was still inside, and at her knock he let her in. "I can only take cash," he said with a bright smile. "Close at seven in the off-season. I know it's easy to get caught up out there."

"I went out to get the cleaner," she said. "Ran into Karol...I forget his last name, now."

Leon frowned and shook his head. "Anton's brother," she went on.

"Oh. Huh." He rested his hands on his hips. "Didn't know he had a brother. But he's pretty close-mouthed, that one. Did you find his place?"

"Yeah, but he wasn't there. I just came by to get some stew for tonight. None of the stuff I bought sounds appetizing any more."

"I know how that is." He laughed. "Why d'you think I own a grocery? Go ahead, grab something. I like Stagg's myself, but we got Dinty Moore and Chunky, too."

"Thanks." She walked down the aisle, nerving herself up for the next part of the conversation. "Oh, I saw a wolf."

Leon didn't say anything, so she went on. "It didn't seem threatening at all. It saw me and..." And it took a bandage off its shoulder, the one I'd dressed, and thanked me for helping it. "And then just vanished."

"They do that, usually," he said. "Hell, I usedta see 'em all the time on the ol' farm, lurkin' in the shadows. More scared of us than we are of them."

"Are they?" She rested her hand on a box of Stagg's Chicken Chili, wondering how the hell she would be able to ask the question she wanted to in this brightly lit grocery store. "It didn't seem all that afraid. I thought maybe there was a wildlife rescue place around here that it could've been released from."

"Ain't nothin' like that around here." She could hear mechanical sounds as he fiddled with the cash register. "Wildlife here gotta fend for itself."

"I also saw that guy in the leather jacket who was in here," she said. "A little earlier."

Leon slammed the cash register shut. "You don't want to have nothin' to do with him."

"I got that." She weighed the box in her hand and then brought it to the front. "He said something, though, about Anton and Karol. I just wanted to ask you about it, if you don't mind."

"Don't trust nothin' that guy says." But he nodded, listening.

"He said they were hired by the police to go after him." She made it a question, tilting her head.

He took the box of chili from her. "Two-fifty."

She dug in her pocket for her wallet. While she did, Leon sighed. "Yeah, the police hired him. Anton was around here already, see. When he heard 'bout the trouble, he told me he could help, and I put him in touch with the sheriff. Didn't know he had a brother, too. But he told me he was working with the sheriff."

She handed him the money. "And they're hunting the wolves."

Leon looked down at the cash in her hand, and then handed her the box. "It's on me," he said. "Don't wanna have to go opening the register. It'll throw my count off."

Valerie put the money on the counter. "Ring it up tomorrow, then." She lifted her head and looked him in the eye. "Are they hunting the wolves?"

His face creased, reddening slightly. "If them wolves would keep to themselves like they ought, this wouldn't never have happened. We thought they didn't want to bother nobody, and we didn't bother them. That's how it always was."

She forced a laugh. "It sounds like you can talk to them."

Leon's laugh sounded as forced as hers. "Well, that's silly, Valerie."

"So what does Breaker have to do with it all?"

"You're best off—"

"Leon."

Their eyes locked. "Right," he said. "Reckon you've heard my advice once. Well, him and his tribe, they live over t'other side of the lake. They... *they* think they can talk to wolves."

"Just *talk* to wolves?"

He stared at her. "You know, Valerie, Annie's gonna be waiting with my dinner. I really should close up here."

She held the box of chili in her hand, gesturing toward him with it. "Why don't you like him and his tribe?"

"This ain't your business." He started to walk out from behind the counter. "Now, I'll see you out—"

All her years in the city told her to let him close up, to take the chili and go. But she had other instincts, from a career in business dominated by men, and that was that when a man told her that it wasn't her problem in that patronizing tone, that there was something behind what he said.

Valerie threw the box of chili at him, hitting him on the arm. Leon jumped and stared at her as she took a step forward, fists clenched. "When a guy shows up on my patio bleeding from a fucking arrow in the shoulder, it's my business. When a wolf sits *waiting for me* outside my house with the same shoulder bandaged, it's my business. When the guy the police hired to help with wolf attacks tells me there are *werewolves* at Lake Wahya, it's my. Fucking. Business."

His expression went from angry to bewildered to resigned, all in the space of her speech. He picked up the box of chili and handed it to her. "Go home," he said, gently. "That's the best thing you can do. Leave this to the town and the tribe."

She shook her head. "I wanted to, but I saved a man's life, and now I'm wondering if I did the right thing. If he's a monster, then I need to make up for it."

"I can't..." He shook his head. "It's complicated."

"Try me." She set the box down on the counter and folded her arms.

Leon took one look at the locked door. "They don't bother nobody. Usually. This year, somethin' changed. That Breaker kid, he was always a wild one. Tribe keeps t'themselves, don't bother us none. Bring us fresh venison once in a while. We barter, like."

"They're Native American?" She recalled Breaker's profile and raven-black hair.

"Iroquois. But Breaker, he's half-and-half, he hangs around and messes with the tourists, sometimes works as a guide, sometimes just talks to 'em."

Her skin prickled. "Sometimes attacks them?"

Leon held up a callused hand. "I ain't sayin' that. But I do know the one girl who died, she came in here the day before, all talkin' about how she seen this big black wolf."

"But she just saw it? It didn't attack her?"

He shook his head, slowly. "Not then. The next day, though…Sheriff said it was a wolf attack."

"Did you ask Breaker?"

He frowned. "I had a yellow dog, years back. She was the sweetest thing…'til she got sick. Then y'never knew from one day to the next if she'd lick your hand or snap at it. Had to put 'er down after she bit Annie." He looked down at the counter. "You just gotta realize they ain't the same anymore."

Valerie shook her head. "I work in the city. I know from crazy. And Breaker's not a dog." She lowered her voice. "You think he's sick?"

Leon's frown deepened. "I dunno what to think," he said. "Exceptin' that you should go home, have your chili, get a good night's rest, and head out in the morning."

Valerie sighed. "If he's sick, Leon, he didn't show it today."

"Today," he said meaningfully.

She shook her head. "I guess you're right." She picked up the box of chili and walked with him to the door, waiting while he unlocked it. Part of her wanted to ask, "do you really believe in werewolves?" but she couldn't bring herself to say the words, and she wasn't sure she wanted to hear his answer, or see his face when she asked.

So she got in her car and drove slowly back up the lakeside road, watching for deer and thinking about Breaker. Had she just been incredibly lucky, back there at the cabin? She'd left the bandage on the ground, hadn't even looked at it as she'd run back out to go to Leon's, but if it was still there, if it was the same one she'd put on Breaker, well, then what? She hoped it would be gone, that she wouldn't have to face it. Because if it was the same one, she would have to admit that the wolf she'd seen was, somehow, insanely, the same as the young man she'd attached it to. As much as her mind wanted to fabricate explanations—Breaker has a tame wolf, he put the bandage on its shoulder—none of those explanations made any sense. As crazy as it was, werewolves were the simplest explanation for everything that had happened.

And that meant that Breaker had probably killed Anton with his own jaws. Valerie bit her lip. So he was probably capable of killing those two girls, too—although a tourist was a very different thing from a hunter coming after you. Still, if he were innocent, why not just go to the police, work with them so they didn't have to call in these two white-coated mercenaries?

Christ, she thought, I'm so glad this is not my problem. I will be happy to get back to Martin and his condescending attitude and I am going to work extra hard on my next proposal, and if I feel dissatisfied at all, I will just say, at least I don't have a suave big game hunter after me, or a werewolf—

She'd turned onto the lane leading up to the cabin, and as she stopped the car, she saw a large, dark shape outlined in the moonlight on the path. Two pointed black ears turned her way as she cut the engine. In a rush, she remembered the other odd thing happening to her here, her newly-discovered rapport with the moon, but there didn't seem to be anything the moon could do right now. Her heart beat faster.

The wolf, sitting up, had something in its mouth. She couldn't quite see what it was in the shadows, from where she was now. She'd have to get out of the car.

Or she could get back in, drive to Geneseo, and stay in a motel overnight. Come back in daylight on her way back to the city. And then she'd never know for sure.

She could get out, leaving the car door open just in case. See how the wolf reacted. Leave herself an out. It hadn't harmed her before, and it wasn't moving now, sitting perfectly still. There was no shine of the moon's reflection in its eyes, but she assumed it was watching her.

The thunk of the car door opening sounded as loud as a hammer to her. The wolf didn't react at all. She pushed the door open and stepped out, slowly, resting one hand on the door.

The night around her seemed to be holding its breath. No sound came of crickets or mice; the air was deathly still. "Breaker?" Her voice trembled, uncertain. Way to be confident, Val, she told herself. Pretend it's the CEO of a customer firm. They can smell fear, too.

She took one more step forward, deciding she'd improvise, and that was when the wolf came at her.

She saw it only as a growing shadow moving impossibly fast. Before she could even take a step backwards, it had covered half the ground between them and had leapt, letting go of the thing in its mouth. She saw this as an incongruous detail, a white flutter dropping to the ground that she would later recognize.

Her feet gave out under her, sending her toppling back into the driver's seat of the car while the large black frame of the wolf slammed into the top of the car, shaking the whole thing, its mouth snapping shut on air where Valerie had been a second before. Time came somewhat back to normal as her hand scrabbled at the door, the wolf just a foot from it shaking off the impact. Her fingers closed around the handle as she got her legs into the footwell, but before she could get it all the way closed, the wolf had pushed its way in, snapping at her and clamping down on her arm.

She screamed and pulled on the door as hard as she could. The heavy door slammed into the wolf's head twice before it staggered back, ripping her shirt sleeve and taking a chunk of flesh from her arm, leaving one paw inside the car. She slammed the door again, feeling the impact on fur and flesh, and this time the wolf yelped. The paw disappeared, and she slammed and locked the door.

Her fingers were shaking too badly to get the key into the ignition. Come on, Val, get it together, she thought, but she couldn't control the trembling. It can't get you any more.

As soon as she said those words to herself, the car shook again and the wolf landed on the hood, glaring through the windshield at her. She screamed again despite herself at the bulk of it, the menacing yellow eyes staring hungrily at her. The immediacy of the terror did what she hadn't been able to do on her own: it steadied her fingers.

The engine turning over filled her with even more confidence. Her blood was still racing, but she felt more in control. "All right, asshole," she said. "You want to go for a ride?" The tough talk was definitely helping. "Fasten your seatbelt, fucker."

She gunned the car in reverse. The wolf skidded, but incredibly stayed on the hood, its claws screeching across the metal. It looked decidedly less threatening, though, giving her even more confidence as she slammed the car into Drive and stomped on the accelerator, turning the wheel to face toward the freeway.

The wolf slammed into her windshield and then slammed into it again, this time under its own power. She could see its snarl now, the teeth bared as it threw its weight against the safety glass. It couldn't crack it, could it? Valerie could only think of a horror movie scenario now, the monster punching through a windshield to drag out the frightened teen inside. "Well," she muttered, "I'm no teen."

At the bottom of the lane, she didn't slow down, swinging the car around hard to the right. The wolf slid almost all the way off the hood, one paw caught in the windshield wiper blade. She could see the white patch in the middle of the black, glowing in the moonlight. "Say goodnight, Gracie," she said, and turned on the wipers.

They rose across the dry glass, and that was enough for the wolf to lose its purchase. It tumbled from the car, landing by the road where the shadows swallowed it up. She kept looking in the rear view mirror, but saw nothing except blackness.

Now the trembling took over again, so bad that she had to stop the car. She was also aware of a growing pain in her arm, but when she looked over, she could only see the torn shirt sleeve in the dark car. Knowing how bad it was would not do anything to help her state of mind. She needed to get somewhere fast, and she didn't dare go back to her cabin, not now.

Movement flickered in front of the car. She jumped in her seat as Breaker appeared in her headlights, his hair wild, eyes wide. He gestured at her, but she couldn't tell what his gestures meant. She was paralyzed. The wolf had fallen off the car, and now here was Breaker. Karol's words came back to her. *One of the worst.*

Clearly frustrated, he came around to her driver's side door and rested his hand against the window. And that spooked her. His lips moved, but she didn't register the words. Her foot slammed down on the gas pedal. Breaker jumped back as the car roared ahead, nearly careening off the road. She didn't look in the rear-view mirror, but she was sure he wasn't following her.

She still didn't know where to go. Her arm was stiff and wet, throbbing with pain. She wasn't sure she could make it to Geneseo; the only other thing she could think to do was drive down to Leon's and lean on the car horn until he came out. But when she rounded a curve in the road and saw a familiar driveway, she remembered: Anton's cabin was right ahead here. And Karol might be there. If he weren't, she didn't have any other plan.

She turned, and almost sobbed in relief when she saw the black pickup parked where it had been that afternoon. She drove past it, up to where lights were showing through the window of the cabin, and stumbled out of the car. The enclosed porch light came on as she pushed through the door. "Karol!" She banged on the door with her right arm, the uninjured one. "Karol, please, I need help."

The door flew open and he stood there, staring, his chiseled face frozen in surprise. Then he put his arm around her shoulder and pulled her inside. "My God, you're bleeding."

She saw the red splashes of blood on the floor. For a moment, it was the conference table again, and Karol was Martin leaning solicitously toward her. The vision passed. Val tried to hold her arm up so it would stop dripping. "Sorry," she said. "It attacked me."

"Come to the kitchen, I have supplies." His words were clipped. He turned quickly and led her to a white, sterile kitchen, where he yanked open a drawer and pulled out a small box. She leaned against the counter; he came over to her and spread out a white cloth. "Lay your arm there."

She obeyed. When he pulled the shirt sleeve gently up, she looked directly at the wound for the first time. It was not as bad as she'd feared, though it was certainly gruesome enough. A couple square inches of skin and flesh had been torn away from the inner forearm, but no major blood vessels had been punctured. Still, the one look was enough. She steeled herself and stared around the kitchen as Karol placed a sterile pad on the arm.

Just as when she'd looked in earlier, there was little indication that anyone was actually living here. The appliances gleamed, the sink showed no signs of dishes or, indeed, that anything had been washed in it recently. The refrigerator was bare, when even the one in Martin's cabin had had magnets attaching emergency numbers and a couple photos. The cupboards, all neatly closed, showed no smudges or stains, so that Valerie wondered if she would find anything in them if she opened them. A stack of spotless dishes, she decided.

"Ow." Something had stung her arm.

"My apologies," he said. "This is an old antiseptic I use. It has never failed to render a wound clean."

"I suppose you would know." She could smell it now, an astringent herbal odor. It wasn't familiar at all, but the pain and the smell reassured her. "My mom always said, if it stings, it's working."

"It is not always so," Karol said. "However, in this case I trust that it is." He wrapped her arm in a gauze bandage and sealed it quickly. The stinging was already fading, taking the pain with it.

"It feels better." She twisted her arm experimentally.

He smiled. "I believe you will survive."

"Yes, I think I will." She felt a little silly now, knowing how minor the injury had been.

His fingers brushed the torn sleeve of her shirt. "You will need a new shirt."

"I have some at my cabin. My jacket's there, too."

"It may be best not to return to your cabin tonight." He looked out the window, then back at her wound. "If that is what it looks like."

"What does it look like?"

He took her wrist in strong fingers, turned the arm to look at the dressed wound. "Wolf," he said.

It wasn't as bad this time, not with him here to steady her against it. "Try 'huge wolf.'" She exhaled. "God, it was...it was waiting for me. Holding..." She stared at her arm, at the gauze bandage. The white thing the wolf had been holding in its mouth: the bandage she'd put on Breaker. "...something, I didn't see what."

"And it attacked?"

She nodded. "As soon as I stepped out of the car."

"He would have killed you." Karol's deep voice echoed in the kitchen. "You are quite fortunate. Perhaps now you understand a little better the danger that stalks the forests here, the perversion of life that seeks only to rend, to destroy."

She gave a quick nod. Intellectually, she knew that wild animals were vicious, but the attack from this one had been so calculating, so planned, that she couldn't help but feel herself buy into Karol's story. And that brought up another question. She poked the wound on her arm gingerly. "If he bit me, does that mean...will I...?"

He smiled. "The legends are somewhat exaggerated. In my experience, a simple bite is never enough to transmit the disease. But we will watch for signs anyway."

His light tone reassured her. "How did you become a hunter?" she asked, suddenly curious. "All the hunters I know wear flannel and camo."

His eyebrow lifted, but he just smiled and gestured to the living room. "Come. You need a different type of medicine, and I will provide a new shirt. I will tell you a story in the meantime. Never fear," he said as she followed him into the neat room, "it is short."

The living room, prim and tidy, nonetheless smelled strongly of the same earthy aroma that she'd noticed on Karol himself, earlier. Either it wasn't present in the kitchen, or she'd been too distracted to catch it. Martin's cabin smelled like furniture polish, though, so she didn't pay much attention. Cabins had weird smells. Probably the basement had a vent going straight up into the living room.

Karol waved her to the plush armchair. On the other side of the room, he opened a small wooden cabinet and poured her a glass of scotch. "I do not like this particular liquor," he said, handing it to her, "but Anton tells me it is fine." Golden highlights winked at her from the silver-rimmed glass.

It was, though not as smooth as what Martin stocked. She needed something more powerful, more raw, so it worked perfectly. She took a sip and set the glass down. "I need to tell you something about your brother," she said.

He sat without betraying any emotion while she told him of seeing Anton die on the island. She couldn't say why she left Breaker completely out of the story; it wasn't completely because she didn't want to own up to having lied earlier in the day. Part of her still remembered the young man she'd met, distinct from the wolf who'd leapt at her just a little while ago, and by not linking him to Anton's death, she kept the two separate for a little while longer.

By the time she'd finished, Karol had moved to stare out the window. "So," he said.

"I'm sorry."

His reflection lowered its eyes to look at her. "Why? You bear no guilt."

Just a little. "For your loss. First your father, now your brother..."

His eyes returned to the dark woods outside. "My father died a long time ago. In the old country." He sighed heavily and sat down. "And my brother's death would not be so tragic had it occurred after our meeting today rather than before. He knew it was a risk to go to the island, but he hoped he could elude the abominations long enough to find out what he needed. It is a setback, I will not deny it."

"What was he looking for?" The scotch got better the more she drank of it.

He returned from the window, sitting on the edge of her armchair. His white pant leg was close enough for her to touch. Not white denim, as Anton had worn, but immaculate linen, she noticed. He must have changed after he got home. Nobody could remain that clean out here. "I have told you about the creatures we are hunting. They are not easy prey. They have allies just as we do." He gestured with a white hand to the window. "Darkness. Forest. The moon. But I think you know something of that."

She covered her guilty start by finishing the scotch. It felt warm in her stomach. "Refill?"

He took the glass and nodded, going to the cabinet to refill it. Valerie looked out of the window, up at the sky, but the moon was nowhere in sight. When Karol returned, he handed her the glass with his left hand, the silver ring on the middle finger gleaming against the gold liquor. "We have managed to tame some of the moon's power," he said, sitting back on the arm of the chair. "Any silver will harm them, but our silver is...assisted. It cannot be removed once it touches the vile flesh. Usually the creature dies within a day. It is often quite painful." His expression, looking over the top of her head, was of someone recalling a fond memory.

"At the time of the full moon, however," he went on, "the abominations may cavort in the open, so protected they are. They engage in their filthy rituals and dances, and though we might be standing as close as you and I are now, we might never see them. However, were we to *know* where these rituals take place, well, then..."

He trailed off. Valerie took another drink. She was starting to feel mildly buzzed, and not a little sleepy. All this discussion of werewolves and magic rituals made perfect sense. "So it takes place on the island?"

Karol shook his head. "The island, surrounded by water, is free of most magic. Venturing there, Anton could see past their protections to discover their secrets. However, his own protections were also annulled, leaving him vulnerable. We agreed he was to go there only as a last resort, and I was to patrol the lake to ensure he was not disturbed. I failed him."

Valerie put a hand on his knee. "You did the best you could, I'm sure." His leg was strong and firm. "Anton wouldn't blame you."

"Of course not," he said. "The creature is to blame. I only regret my inability to finish the job."

Guilt attempted to flower in Valerie's gut, but the warmth of the scotch repressed it. "There was something in his wallet," she said.

Karol looked sharply at her. She blinked. "Didn't I say I found his wallet?"

"No," he said, carefully.

"I'm sorry." She waved a hand. "I felt guilty taking it, I guess. There was some money in it, and a piece of paper with a location written on it. I guess you should have it." She giggled. "I keep guessing. I'm sorry."

He shook his head. "Never mind. Where is it now?"

She frowned. "It's in my jacket. No, wait. It's..." She had taken it out, and put it in something. "In the kitchen? In the bedroom? I'm sorry, I can't really remember."

"Tomorrow, we can go." Karol's face had grown gentler, though his voice still sounded harsh. "You will need to sleep tonight."

"You promised me a story," she protested, glad he wasn't more upset at her.

"Indeed." He rose and walked into the next room. "Can you hear me?"

She nodded, then felt silly. "Yes," she called.

She heard him opening drawers. "I am from a small town whose name you would not recognize. It was burned to the ground in one of the many wars my country has suffered. My family had farmed the land for generations. It was a grant from King Jagiello for faithful service to the crown. There were lean years and bountiful years, but our family always survived."

She closed her eyes. She could see him there, in his white suit, and the mention of the king brought the image to her of him wearing a simple silver crown, smiling regally. "My brother and I were born under a harvest moon, five years apart. It was said to be lucky to have one child born to the harvest moon, let alone two. But it spelled doom for our family.

"When I turned fifteen, a young girl in our village was killed. We thought it was just the wolves, though they had never troubled us before. A month later, another was killed. It took a year before we understood that a plague had descended on our village. My father was one of those who undertook to scourge it, and he was one who lost his life." He emerged from the bedroom with a long-sleeved white cotton shirt.

Valerie thought he looked tired, though his eyes still burned with cold fire. "Did they succeed?"

He draped the shirt over the arm of the chair. "After a fashion. The plague was banished from our village. Years later, though, we would hear that it had sprung up again elsewhere. Our tools were ineffective; we succeeded only in convincing them that the prey was easier elsewhere."

"So you didn't kill them?" She fingered the material of the shirt. It was cool cotton, but sturdy. Good simple clothing.

"Regrettably, no. Not at that time." He flexed his fingers. "But we learned."

She couldn't help staring at the ring. Its soft silver light penetrated even though her heavy eyelids. "You tamed the moon."

"We allied ourselves with a powerful benefactor, who has an interest in keeping the laws of nature intact."

His words were coming from further and further away. "It's good to have powerful friends," she murmured. "That's how you get ahead."

He rested a hand on her shoulder. "You should sleep. You may take the bedroom."

"Mm." She got up, groggily. "Where will you sleep?"

He gestured to the couch. "I need little sleep these days. The facilities are just down the hall, should you need to make use of them. Please, take your rest."

She remembered getting up and swaying, and then his strong hands on her shoulders, sliding down her arms and guiding her to the bed. She pulled her shirt off—or did he—and inhaled the strong, earthy smell of him. It wasn't that objectionable. When she and Steven used to work in the garden together, before she got wrapped up in work and he got wrapped up in Beverly, that was a good smell, a healthy feeling, going along with pleasant exhaustion and a sense of harmony. They would come in from the garden and shower together, making love in the shower, or else they would lie in the bed, clean and naked, and make love slowly, hands traveling over each others' bodies, sharing that same togetherness.

Of course, with Steven it had all been an illusion. Karol's hands moved over her shoulders, down to her sport bra, and she thought for a moment he would try to undo it, but he did not, just moved down the curve of her back, his fingers chilly against her dried sweat. She leaned her head against his shoulder.

"I know what is best," he assured her. "I will keep you safe."

She nodded. "I feel safe." It was the right thing to say, not actually how she felt, but as she said it she felt it become more true. He was solid, not like an oak, but like a smooth white birch tree. His whispers to her faded into the rustle of birch leaves. She circled his waist with her arms and felt the shadow of the black wolf recede, until its

—his—

eyes were no more than a distant spot of light.

Karol bent to murmur in her ear, his breath soft as an evening breeze. "Tonight, you should sleep."

What a gentleman, she thought. She couldn't even feel anything against her hip, nothing that would have prompted her to try to take more clothes off, in her half-asleep buzz. So she let his strong hands guide her to the edge of the bed.

She remembered lying down on the bed without even pulling the sheet over herself, lying there in her bra and jeans. But those memories were disconnected, all jumbled in with other memories like fragments of dreams.

And she remembered Karol sitting on her bed, murmuring words while holding her shirt. Beyond him, outside the room, she could see

Breaker standing there even though there was no window. He was angry with her, but desperate at the same time. In his hands, he held the arrow she'd pulled from him. She saw, distinctly, a drop of blood collect at the tip. And then Karol was stroking her arm with his fingers, brushing the wound dressing, his touch on her skin chilling, but also somehow reassuring. And through the ceiling she could see the sky, but it was totally dark. When she looked over again, Breaker was gone. And Karol was gone, too, and the room was empty and dark.

Mother Moon, she murmured in her sleep, aware that she was dreaming, Mother Moon, where are you?

That was very rude, Karol was saying from somewhere. But the moon was there, a silver circle in the sky where his head should have been. It shone down on her, but instead of illuminating the room, it illuminated sounds, a low murmuring she could hear that she hadn't before, like the whisper of leaves in the wind. And the moon was hollow, a thin circle of silver with black at its center. Where's the heart, she whispered to herself, and she felt Karol's fingers on her breast, though she couldn't see him anywhere. Here, here, here, he said, but his voice was rougher, darker, and it wasn't his voice after all.

Ask the moon for help, it said.

She tossed and turned. She didn't want to be rude, did she? Karol was keeping her safe, and there was no need for any other help. But there was something wrong with the moon, the hollow moon, and the wrongness sat inside her, cold and empty. She needed more liquor to warm her.

The taste of the scotch came back to her, the golden liquid and the warmth it had spread through her. She had the sense of sleeping in a cocoon, a golden haze around her, but it did nothing to drive away the cold.

Ask the moon for help.

The moon can't help me, not without its heart. She was no stranger to coldness, to emptiness in her bed, not lately. Steven had said he would protect her, too. He'd thought he'd known what was best for her. And in the early days, he had placed his hand on her breast, and it had been warm, so warm. She felt again the ghostly fingers on her breast, though there was no voice this time. She knew what he wanted her to do, and Steven wouldn't be happy with it.

Steven wasn't happy at all these days, not until he'd shown up with the papers. And why should she care about him anyway? But how did she know she could trust anyone?

The only one who hadn't presumed to know what was best for her was Breaker. The only one who hadn't asked her to trust him was Breaker. He had chosen to place his trust in her. He had told her to ask the Moon for help.

Rudeness be damned. "Mother Moon, help me."

She heard her voice, in the way you hear yourself cry out when waking from a nightmare, as though it were someone else's. Sparks crackled the length of her body, down through her breasts and loins, to the tips of her toes. Silver radiance blossomed behind her eyelids, nearly unbearable. She sat up abruptly in bed, opened her eyes.

Outside the window of the room she lay in, the moon glowed brightly, bathing her in its light. The house was still. No shapes moved outside, and Karol was not in the room anywhere that she could see.

No; the house was not completely still. She could hear something now, a faint susurration of words. The strange thing was that she wasn't hearing them with her ears. When she turned her head, the sound of them didn't change. They were coming from...from outside? From below?

She stood. The stillness of the house enfolded her, but it was a cold stillness and it raised goosebumps on her arms. She picked up Karol's white cotton shirt and slipped it on, rubbing her arms for comfort more than warmth, the sturdy fabric rough under her fingers. On impulse, she walked to the dresser and opened the top drawer.

It was empty. So was the drawer below it. So, when she walked over to open it, was the closet. Valerie looked out the window at the moon as if to say, you see this, mother? What the hell? She walked to the doorway and peered into the living room, half-expecting to see Karol lying on the couch with his hands folded over his chest, like a blanched vampire. But he was not in the living room at all.

"I'm starting to get a bad feeling about this," she murmured to herself. The whole living room was as quiet and neat as if this were a model home, not the house of a man who'd had his arms around her just a few hours ago. The kitchen, too, was spotless, even the white towel with its spots of red put away somewhere.

The only place she'd seen any sign that someone actually lived here was the basement, and the only door inside the house that wasn't open or a closet was in the kitchen: a white door, firmly shut, smelling strongly of earth and plants, but not of mildew, as she would expect from a cellar. She turned the knob and pulled, but it was locked. "Basements don't lock from the inside," she muttered, and started opening kitchen drawers.

The key was in the bottom drawer closest to the sink. She hefted it with some satisfaction. "Can't ask the moon for everything," she said as she fitted it to the lock and turned it.

It made a loud thunk as the bolt shot back, but after a moment of waiting, nothing else had moved, so she eased the door open gently. Behind it, she saw a flight of wooden stairs leading down into darkness. The smell of loam, of growing things, was overpowering.

The light switch just inside the door illuminated the stairs. She crept down them cautiously. "Karol?" she called, but there was no reply.

The basement was just as she'd seen it through the window. Fully a third of it was taken up by the garden, which she could now see was not only wheat, but also corn and some low green plants she didn't recognize. She reached out to touch the stalks of wheat. They felt real, all right. She resisted the temptation to break off one of the delicate leaves, and instead walked over to the workbench.

Here, something was different, and it wasn't just the rankness of the odor, a sharper smell than just the dirt and plants. The circles of rocks and teeth she'd seen from the window had been empty, but now there was something in the center of one: a paper cup with the Starbucks logo on it. Her skin prickled. She reached out to pick it up, and the smell of cappuccino overwhelmed her. There was the little crease her thumbnail always made in her coffee cups when she held them.

Oh, God. It was her cup. He'd kept it from Starbucks, not thrown it away. And then he'd brought it here to do what? Her eyes strayed to the line of glass jars, the size of the Mason jars her mother had preserved fruit in. Only two of them contained anything. Hands trembling, she picked up one and held it to the light.

It held a scrap of cloth, white with green checks, and a decorative fringe. It looked like it had come from a woman's blouse. Valerie set it back down and picked up the second jar, but its contents were no less illuminating: a small lipstick, dark red, with fingerprints visible on it.

She set it down. Her heart pounded when she looked at the Starbucks cup again. Had he used it to send her into some kind of stupor, when she'd thought she was just drunk on Scotch? She bent to look more closely at it, still loath to touch it.

The teeth that surrounded it looked too large to be human. They lay carefully arranged with the points facing inward, some of them large shearing teeth, others incisors, and one—one was a long canine tooth. A fang.

The rocks, between the teeth, were not rocks. They were clods of earth, but it was from them that the rank smell came. It smelled like...like...

—a black paw, jaws snapping in the moonlight—

The image came to her like a flash. She jerked her head back and caught a flash of white out of the corner of her eye, through the window. The moon would be a welcome sight right now, she thought, so she stood on tiptoe to peer out.

The white was not the moon. It was Karol's white suit. He was crouched on the ground outside, waving something bunched in one hand at a shape in front of him. The shape moved, resolving out of the shadows into the form of a large black wolf.

Valerie sucked in a breath that she hoped they couldn't hear. She couldn't hear anything they were doing, and Karol was definitely talking. The wolf had its ears back and was limping, cowering as Karol waved the thing in his hand at it. Valerie watched, spellbound, as Karol cuffed the wolf across the muzzle, and although the thing could have ripped his throat out, it just took it like Benjy had when Steven hit him.

Karol threw the cloth in his hands to the ground and stood, glaring down at the wolf. It turned and started to slink away. Valerie watched until it occurred to her that Karol was very likely going to come back into the house, and then she hurried to the stairs and ran up as quietly as she could. The kitchen was still silent, and she didn't hear the front or back door open, so she re-locked the basement and replaced the key. Just as she was sliding the drawer shut, she did hear the soft click of the back door latch.

She reached for one of the cabinets at random and opened it. A stack of bright white plates stared her in the face, so like what she'd imagined being there that she almost started giggling. She had closed it and reached for another one when Karol's voice sounded behind her. "Can I help you find something?"

"I was thirsty," she said.

He strode to a cabinet on the other side of the kitchen and handed her a glass from it. "The water in the sink is good."

She filled the glass, proud of how steady her hands were. "You weren't in the living room."

"I told you I do not sleep much." His voice was slightly sharp, his eyes narrow. "I enjoy walking in the woods. They are peaceful at night."

What kind of peace, she wondered. "You'll have to take me around and show me sometime."

"Perhaps later." He rested a hand on her shoulder and pushed her gently out of the kitchen. "You have had a stressful night and you should be sleeping. In the morning, we can go back to your cabin."

"I might be okay to go back now." She didn't think it would work, but she had to try it.

He shook his head, following her into the bedroom. "I do not think that would be advisable. Not until it is light."

"There's plenty of light from the moon."

His brow lowered. "Indeed," he said. "I fear that is what is keeping you awake." He closed the curtains over the window, and though Valerie didn't quite see what he was doing, she could swear he made a little hand motion when he did so. Immediately she felt a chill, so she sat on the bed and pulled the blankets up over her.

Karol brushed the side of his white jacket, now muted in the dark room. "Sleep well, Valerie," he said. "I will see you in the morning."

Though cold, she was much more clear-headed when she lay down this time. Even with the blankets, she never quite got warm, but she did eventually fall asleep.

Chapter 8

She wouldn't have known it was morning if Karol hadn't knocked at the door. He opened it and came in without waiting for an answer.

Valerie had been lying awake for perhaps fifteen minutes, turning over the previous day's events in her head and trying to make sense of it all. No matter how she turned it over, she couldn't. All she could figure was that she wanted to get the hell out of this place and away from all of its creepy locals as soon as she could, back to the city where at least the junkies looked like junkies, and they didn't turn into wolves or talk to wolves or conduct rituals with her trash in their basement.

Karol's appearance in her room, a bizarre mix of televangelist and bed-and-breakfast owner as he threw open the curtains in his white suit, did nothing to comfort her. He had resumed the false cheer he'd had at their first meeting. How had she ever confided in him, leaned against him the previous night, put her arms around him and wished, however fleetingly, that he would join her in bed? The scotch *must* have been drugged.

"It is a beautiful morning," he said, flooding the room with light. "Would you like to freshen up before we leave?"

He was smiling as though the previous night had not happened. Still, the thought of being naked in his bathroom was distinctly unappealing now. "Just a couple minutes," Valerie said. "Oh, do you have my shirt?"

Karol dropped his eyes to her chest. "Is that shirt not suitable?"

"I don't want to wear my shirt, I just want to take it back."

He nodded. When she came out of the bathroom, he was holding it bunched up in his hand, and he held it out to her. She froze, recognizing the gesture, suddenly certain that this shirt was what he'd been holding out to the wolf the night before. "Do you not want this?"

"No, I do." She took it quickly. When his back was turned, she brought it to her nose, but she couldn't tell if the dirt smell was from dirt on the shirt or was just Karol's earthy scent permeating everything in the house. She kept the shirt in her hand, walking behind him to the front of the house.

Although she was hungry, she didn't ask for food, and he didn't offer. When they walked out into the sunlight, he walked to his truck and placed a hand on her shoulder when she started past it, to her car. "It would be more convenient to take one vehicle."

"Oh," she said, "I don't want you to have to drive me back here when we're done. I'll just stay at the cabin."

"Hm." He nodded, briefly, but she was already walking past him. The nerve, acting as though it was on his say-so that she would be allowed to drive her own car. She got in, pleased to find there was no flashback to the wolf attack of the previous night. In the sunshine, the whole episode would have felt like a dream if not for the bandage under the unfamiliar shirt sleeve on her arm.

Valerie found herself driving faster along the narrow lakeside road, not even slowing for the cars they passed. Karol kept up with her well at first, then began to fall back during the winding curves her small sedan was able to take faster than his pickup. She didn't need much lead time—maybe about twenty seconds—but she'd already determined that whatever information was on that paper in his brother's wallet, she didn't want him to have it any more. Seriously, what was it with men? Stephen had been inconsiderate, selfish, arrogant, but at least he'd never set a wolf to try to kill her.

She flew up the lane to the cabin and slammed on the brakes. Not bothering to lock the car door, she reached the front door of Martin's cabin (making sure it didn't look like she was running) and stepped inside just as Karol's truck pulled up behind her car. It took her a moment to find the right drawer in the kitchen; he stepped into the entryway as she was opening it and removing the small folded piece of paper. On impulse, she took the broken arrow from the counter and jammed it into her pocket with the paper, in case he recognized it as his brother's and asked where she'd gotten it.

"Here you go," she said. "And your arrow is there, if you want it."

He glanced at his arrow, the intact one, but only for a moment, his fingers already working at the wallet. He rifled through the cash and then looked up at her. "There is only money here. You said there was something else."

"Sure there is." She affected surprise, taking the wallet back to look for herself. "It's right here, behind the—oh."

He met her eyes when she looked up. "What?"

"Well," she said softly, "Breaker was here, and I was out running errands. He probably saw me put the wallet away and took the paper out of it."

It sounded convincing enough to her. Karol took the wallet back and tapped it against his palm, finally slipping it into a suit pocket and nodding. "That is unfortunate," he said. "Do you happen to remember anything about the paper?"

"He'd written numbers on it," she said. "Six and eight, I think." She tried to remember whether she'd told him anything specifically about the piece of paper.

"Hm." He rubbed his fingers together and then picked up the arrow. "I will need this."

She frowned, not making the connection, not sure whether there was one. "I'm sorry it's not there. And I do very much appreciate all your help last night. It was pretty frightening."

His expression changed, focused on her with a suave smile again. "I can imagine," he said. "These creatures are terrible things."

She shuddered. "I hope I never see it again. I'm going to get out of here today and go back home."

Karol paused. He put one hand to the side of his face. "If you would like to help me," he said slowly, "it would be most appreciated if you could remain for just one more day."

Valerie frowned. "One day?"

"Yes. I believe that the creature 'Breaker' has developed an attraction to you. If you remain here, the chance that he will seek you out again is high."

For a moment, she flashed back to Breaker lying on her living room floor, jacket open to his taut, bare stomach. Then she remembered the wolf leaping at her as she fell back into the car. She shuddered. "I'm not sure I can handle that."

"I will be nearby," he said.

Then she understood. "You want to use me as *bait*?"

He held up his hand. "You will be in no danger. I promise."

Valerie folded her arms. She opened her mouth to argue, but it occurred to her that the quickest way to get him to go away would be to agree. She'd seen him talking to the wolf last night, and she didn't trust him any further than she could throw him. "Well," she said, "if you promise to keep me safe."

She thought there was something wolfish in his smile. "I do," he said.

After he'd gone, she locked the door. Then she ransacked her cupboard for anything appropriate for breakfast. Cramming two Pecan Sandies into her mouth and carrying three more in her hands, she wandered out to the living room and immediately wished she hadn't. Not only did she stub her toe on the steam cleaner, which she'd left sitting in the doorway, but the sight of the bloodstain, now dried into the carpet, gave the cookies in her mouth a bad taste. She hadn't cleaned the outside window, either, but at least that stain wasn't as noticeable.

She hurried out onto the deck and finished her cookies there, looking out over the lake. It was hard to believe that such beautiful scenery concealed such terrible things. The trees just fringed with yellow curved down to the calm blue of the lake, which stretched out to the darker green across the way. Just watching the birds soar back and forth between the trees, the wind rippling the surface of the water, and the clouds gathering leisurely above her calmed her. She licked the crumbs from her fingers and went back inside, determined to clean up the carpet and then get in her car and leave.

Cleaning up a large bloodstain with a steam cleaner turned out to be more gruesome to smell than to watch. The chemicals in the steam already made the cookies in her stomach churn; as they mixed with the blood in the fibers, the smell got worse. The carpet was still discolored when she was done, but she'd tell Martin she'd spilled wine. Or something.

She had just unplugged the steam cleaner when the hair stood up on the back of her neck. That feeling she'd had the previous afternoon, walking up to the cabin, was back. Slowly, she turned and looked out onto the patio.

The black wolf sat there, staring at her through the blood-smeared glass. As she watched, it licked its lips, slowly.

She'd locked the patio door, hadn't she? She felt for the car keys in her pocket. There was no way it could get around the house in time if she ran now. Quick as the thought occurred to her, she sprinted through the foyer, unlocked the front door with shaking hands, and ran down the path.

Her car sat parked where she'd left it. She dug in her pocket for the keys, to unlock it, but found the arrow instead. She pulled it out just as a heavy weight hit her in the side and she went tumbling to the dirt. The smell of the wolf overwhelmed her, the rich earthy musk of it bringing back her terror of the night before. She struggled against its weight, trying to throw it off, but it locked its teeth around her arm, right where it had bitten her last night, and she screamed.

It was growling at her, a bass rumble low in its throat that would have been terrifying even if it hadn't been on top of her. "Oh God," she moaned, "get away, get off, get off!" Her hand holding the arrow was trapped under her. The wolf let go of her arm and lunged, but she brought the arm up to block it and got another bite, lower down. She could see in the flashes of the white shirt and black wolf that spun back and forth above her that she was bleeding again, drops of red splattering the white shirt.

The arrow, beneath her, dug into her side. The wolf growled, trying to shake free of her arm. Valerie closed her eyes and tried to twist her body to free her other arm, but the wolf's weight was too much. She brought up a leg and kicked as it bit at her again, this time tearing the shirt and another piece of her arm.

The arm fell to her side, the wolf letting it go. It drew back to lunge again, and in that moment she twisted herself around. Her free arm came up with the arrow and stabbed it in the chest, just in front of the shoulder.

The wolf let out a yelp, and almost immediately the pressure on her eased. It stumbled to one side, turning its head toward the shaft buried in its black fur. Valerie got up to a sitting position and scooted back, not trusting her legs to get up yet. Her hand closed around a small rock, so she threw it at the wolf's head, aware as she did so what a small gesture it was.

But it seemed to spark the wolf to action. It yelped again, looked at her, and then limped quickly away into the trees.

OhGodOhGodOhGodOhGod. Valerie's left arm was a bloody mess, the shirt shredded, the carefully applied bandage from the night before hanging by one piece of tape, skin in pieces, blood soaking the white cotton shirt. *That could be my throat*, she thought, and immediately turned to the side and heaved up the cookies she'd just eaten.

Back in the house, she thought numbly. First aid, water. Then get in the car and get the hell away from here. She struggled to her feet and half-ran to the open door, pushing it closed behind her. In the kitchen, she turned the faucet on full, pulled up her sleeve, and shoved her arm under it. Deep breaths, she told herself. You can do this. You're safe. Nobody can get in.

She took one deep breath, and then a voice from the living room said, "That was well done."

Water and blood splashed all over the kitchen floor as she whirled around. Breaker was leaning in the doorway between the kitchen and living room, smiling. He started toward her, arms outstretched.

Her fingers splayed across the counter in search of a weapon, but Karol had taken his other arrow. She grabbed her car keys from her pocket and stuck them between her fingers, brandishing the fist at him. "You stay back," she said.

He stopped. "I was ready to rescue you. Readier than I was last night—sorry about that. I guess I scared you."

"What?" The white of his face in the glare of her headlights came back, the movement of his lips outside her window, his frantic expression. "Rescue me? I—"

"You did really well," he said quietly, and he looked like he wanted to reach out for her, but she was still brandishing the car keys at him. She lowered her hand, somewhat embarrassed.

"I was terrified." The word seemed too small to describe the feelings she'd gone through.

He stepped forward again, and this time she let him. His hands, warm and strong, rested on her shoulders. "You survived last night and this morning. You did very well this morning. Used his own weapons against him."

"Him?"

"The hunter. Well, his creature, anyway."

She stared at his untidy raven hair, the slight smile on his face, his casual pose. She wanted to put her arms around him, but needed to know. "Let me see your shoulder."

He laughed and released her, turning as he shrugged his jacket down to his elbows so she could see his back. She examined the sharp shoulder blades, the strong muscles showing in graceful curves around the ridge of his spine. Not only was there no sign of the broken arrow shaft, there was not even any trace of the injury she'd treated just the previous day, the one she'd just cleaned up after.

"Satisfied?"

"Yes." Her throat was dry. He turned around, giving her a view of his broad, toned chest before shrugging the jacket back up. "That...wasn't you."

He shook his head. "Not me."

"Oh God." She leaned forward, put her arms around him. He smelled like leather and sweat, the pine of the forest and the raw, clean air of the lake, and he felt as good as she'd imagined, warm and solid and real. "Then...you're not a werewolf."

The word spilled out before she could stop it. Abashed, she let out a sharp laugh, which was cut short as she saw the thin line of his pursed lips, the lowered eyebrows and the movement of his eyes, away from her, down to the counter.

"Well," he said, "since you mention it. Yes, I am."

Chapter 9

Valerie let go. He didn't look at her as she stepped back, but she stared at him until he raised his brown eyes. "That isn't funny," she said.

He spread his hands. "Mother always said I have no comic timing."

"I'm serious."

"So am I." He shrugged. "I love watching comedies, I just can't make the jokes."

Oh, he was doing that thing. "Stop it!"

He nodded once, sharply. "You'd better get that arm bandaged up. Where's the kit you had yesterday?"

"You can't just say 'I'm a werewolf' and then offer to bandage my arm." She held the arm up, blood still dripping from it.

"Why not?" She saw the corner of his mouth twitch upward. "Your arm needs bandaging, and I am a—"

"You just can't." She sighed and then tilted her head toward the cupboard. "In there."

He found the kit and brought it to the counter. "Wow, it got you good. Could be worse, though."

"Could have been a silver arrow?" His hands were warm and reassuring on her arm. She started to relax.

"That wouldn't have mattered much to you. But I'm sure it didn't like it much." He took a sterile pad and dabbed at the wound. Valerie winced, but his fingers were gentle and the pain fleeting, not like the stinging when Karol had applied his whatever to it yesterday. She was oddly glad that that wound had been uncovered and that Breaker was re-dressing it.

"What...was it?" She shook her head at his amused smile. "I mean, besides a big, scary wolf."

"Isn't that enough?" He wound the gauze around her arm.

She hesitated. "I saw him talking to it last night."

Breaker stopped for a moment, then went on, keeping his attention focused on the bandaging. "I didn't know," he said. "I suspected."

"Is it just a wolf?"

He shook his head, sharply. "It is nothing I have seen before. Did it get you anywhere else?"

"No. Just the arm." He'd stopped wrapping, though his hand lingered there. Valerie looked down and saw her arm almost mummified in bandages. She moved it experimentally. "Thanks."

He pulled the arm back. "I don't want to see you hurt any more. Besides, I owed you one. Still do, I reckon."

"Well, I couldn't let you die on the patio." Looking out into the living room, she could see the bloody glass of the patio window. She craned her neck and saw that the door was open an inch. Her blood froze. "Oh, God..."

She ran into the living room, feet squelching on the wet carpet. The room was empty, and so was the patio. She slammed the door closed and locked it, glaring out at the trees. "It was out there."

Breaker coughed, behind her. "Uh," he said, sounding so embarrassed that she turned to look at him. "It wasn't, actually."

"I saw it." She kept looking down toward the lake. No canoes or kayaks broke its surface, even though the sun was higher now and Sammy's place must be open. "It was sitting right here."

"Not the wolf that attacked you." He walked up to stand beside her.

"You can't possibly know. You weren't here."

He didn't answer until she turned to see his half-smile, apologetic. "I thought you'd understood. I thought you knew."

Valerie folded her arms, then unfolded them hurriedly as the bandages rubbed raw skin underneath. "You." He nodded. Her heart beat faster. "But it wasn't you that attacked me." He shook his head. She took a deep breath. "Okay," she said. "Prove it."

That startled him. "Now?" She nodded, curtly. "Well, I'd have to...I mean, my clothes don't..."

She gestured to the patio. "What were you going to do earlier? Ask me to turn my back in wolf sign language?" Part of her clung to the familiar solidity of the woods and the lake and the sun, believing that this upstate rebel was playing a joke on her. But having seen the silver arrows, having been attacked by a wolf, having spent the night with a creepy Eastern European hunter, that part's voice had grown fainter over the last day. The rest of her waited for this confirmation that the reality she knew was just the surface, that there were things lurking beneath that she'd never glimpsed nor guessed at.

"I...wasn't going to talk to you. Not then. I was just glad to see you alive."

"It looked like 'you' wanted to eat me."

He rolled his eyes. "My tail was wagging. Don't you know anything about wolves?"

"All I saw was teeth and a tongue," she said. "And you're still not proving it."

He held her eyes and then gave another shrug, slipping his jacket off his bare shoulders. "Open the door."

"This one?" She reached for the patio door.

"I'll go out there. You can lock the door after me. Don't want you to be frightened again." He dropped the leather jacket onto the couch and rested his thumbs in the waist of his jeans. She could see the white waistband of his underwear beneath them.

Without another word, she unlocked the door and slid it open. He smiled at her and stepped out onto the deck, facing the lake. His hands moved to his jeans, undoing the fastening, and then he pushed them down, muscles bunching in his back as he stepped out of the jeans and left them puddled on the wooden deck.

Valerie's heart beat faster. She almost turned away, but then Breaker glanced over his shoulder, just a quick, sly look to make sure she was watching. He stood still for a moment, showing off, she was sure, and he had a lot to show off. His body reminded her of an athlete's, coiled energy visible in each muscle.

She could see the shape of his body well enough that when he did drop his underwear, with the quick casualness of a locker room, nothing about it was surprising. But it was beautiful, even the dark hair running thickest along his spine, ending just above those taut cheeks, where there definitely was not a tail. He shifted his weight from one leg to the other and leaned forward against the railing. His whole body tensed, as though he'd seen something below, but his head was lifted to the sky as though in pain.

Lost in admiring his body, she almost didn't notice the thickening of the hair. It crept down his arms in a black wave that shimmered in the sunlight, her first indication that this was really happening. Fascinated, she stared as hair lengthened into fur, covering the lean muscular lines but not hiding them completely. There was now, she saw, a tail. Just a small one, but it covered the cleft between his buttocks, inching downward as she watched.

His body changed next, smoothly and easily. The spine pushed up from the back, shoulders and hips moving down to assume a more lupine profile, while his thighs contracted into powerful pistons set alongside his hips, and his ankles lengthened into the lower part of his legs. The hand she could see folded in on itself, fingers withdrawing into solid black-furred paws.

And now his head turned in profile to her, still raised to the sky, elongated into a muzzle. His tongue hung out of the side of his mouth and his triangular ears were cupped forward, and when he opened his eyes, he smiled widely. He was not straining to the sky in pain, she understood, but in pleasure. For a moment, her body ached with the curiosity of what that must feel like, the rearranging and reshaping to become something else, while keeping the essence of yourself.

Breaker dropped to all fours. She had seen him change; she could not deny that it was him. Standing on the wooden deck, the large black wolf stretched in very much the same way Benjy used to, and then tilted its—his—head at her, panting slightly with a grin that made it look like he was laughing. She rested her hand on the door latch, still uncertain about letting him in, flashbacks of the attacks bursting across her memory.

But he was standing patiently, watching her, waiting for a reaction. She smiled and lifted a hand, and he lifted his ears. She had the impression that he was grinning.

It was hard to make her hand pull the door. Intellectually, she knew she should let him back in, but her hindbrain was yelling, *What if he turns savage in wolf form? You could just get to the car and run now, never have to deal with any of this again.*

The memory of her last run to the car came back to her. Then Breaker put a paw forward, and she saw what her mind had missed: his paw was solid black. She saw again the distinct white spot on the paw of the wolf that had attacked her, and only as she pulled the door open did it occur to her that it had been across the base of one digit of the paw, like a silver ring.

Breaker had just stepped forward again when his ears shot up. He darted forward, into the living room, and Valerie jumped back in surprise. She heard a clatter and saw something flash by the window, arcing across the deck where Breaker had stood a moment before and disappearing into the woods on the other side.

I won't be far, Karol had said. She slammed the door closed and locked it again. The living room was now empty. "Breaker?"

A low growl answered her, from the kitchen. She stepped cautiously onto the tiled floor and saw the black wolf standing, ears alert and focused on the living room. "Can you understand me?" she asked.

He looked at her and nodded, unmistakably, then resumed his vigil. "I locked the door," she said, and then she hurried to the front door and threw the latch there, too. Breaker relaxed only a little when both locks were thrown, keeping his eyes focused on the patio. Valerie picked up the phone. "I'm going to call the police. Tell them he's shooting..."

Breaker looked up at the phone in her hand. "It's dead." She jiggled the button. "No signal."

She wasn't sure how a wolf would show surprise, but she was pretty sure Breaker wasn't. "Would you turn back so we can talk about how to get out of here?"

He looked out at the patio again, not glaring, just looking, and gave a soft "whuff." Valerie followed his gaze and saw his jeans and underwear. She put a hand to her mouth, stifling a giggle. "Oh, you're all modest now?"

He tossed his head and assumed a dignified pose. She grinned and then took her cell phone out, but it still had no service. There had to be some way for them to get out. Maybe if one of them distracted him, the other could run to the car...

She looked down in surprise to find Breaker tugging on the cuff of her jeans. "Hey!"

He let go immediately, looked up at her with a grin, and grasped the cuff of the other leg and pulled. "Oh, what, you'll change back if I take *my* clothes off?"

He sat up at that, grinning with his tongue hanging out. "I bet you would," she muttered, trying not to show how strongly the idea appealed to her. "There's a maniac outside shooting magic arrows at us, and you want to get naked." The wolf's silly grin made her laugh, finally. "I'll go into the bedroom and see if Martin left any clothes here."

Breaker padded after her as she investigated the closet, which held only linens, and the dresser, which was empty except for a folded pile of denim. She thought it was jeans, but when she shook it out in front of him, it turned out to be a pair of faded overalls. Breaker eyed it and shook his head firmly.

"It's the only thing in the house." She tried to hide her smile. He turned his head, looking back out at the living room and the patio. "You don't want to go out there. He'll shoot you again. And I'm tired of pulling arrows out of you."

He laid his ears back and lay down, crossing his forelegs and flopping his muzzle on top of them. She took that to be acceptance. "I'll just wait out here," she said with a smile, and closed the door on her way out.

While he was changing, silently, she stood in the living room and listened. The arrow had come from around the side of the house, but Karol could easily have moved, or still be moving. Even if he'd only tried to kill her as a way to lure Breaker into the open, he'd still tried to kill her. She'd seen him holding out her shirt to the wolf, the same wolf that had attacked her outside the cabin. Breaker might be

—a werewolf—

a bit standoffish, but at least he didn't hoard her trash, or give her drugged scotch (it must have been drugged, right?). And it was pretty clear to her that it hadn't been him who'd killed those other girls.

The bedroom door opened. "So what did happen—" She turned around and couldn't stifle the giggle at the sight of him in the overalls. They were tight on his broad frame, and small, ending just above his ankles. The look he gave her, full of wounded pride, just made her giggle more. "I'm sorry, I'm sorry."

"I'm getting my jeans back," he huffed. He took a fireplace poker and stalked to the patio door.

"It won't reach," Valerie told him, though she enjoying watching him crouch in the overalls. "Is your dignity really worth an arrow in the side?"

The tip of the poker fell a full two feet short of where he'd left the jeans. He lay flat on the floor, carefully extending his arm out over the wooden boards. Valerie crouched behind him. "Seriously," she said. "Be careful."

He grunted in reply, pushing the poker out until his head was just at the edge of the door. Valerie grabbed his shoulder. "That's far enough."

Breaker tried to pull away from her, but she wrestled him back. "If you stick your head out there, you think he can resist that target? You think he wants to shoot you in the arm again?"

That stopped him. He lifted his nose and made a noncommittal noise, but pulled the poker back in. He tossed it back near the fireplace, put on his leather jacket, and sat on the living room carpet, trying several positions before crossing his legs beneath him. The overalls rode up almost to the middle of his calf. Valerie closed and locked the patio door, then sat with her knees drawn up. "So," he said. "Any bright ideas?"

She raised her eyebrows. "It would help if I knew what we were dealing with."

He gazed past her. "You likely know more than I do."

"You told me to call the moon for help," she pointed out. "And he said something about taming the moon."

His brow darkened. "I know they don't sleep much."

"That's reassuring."

"It's hard to hurt them. You can tear their throat out, and they get back up again."

Valerie looked out to the lake. "Except on the island."

The black wolf was momentarily evident in his grin. "That felt good."

"You knew he was vulnerable there."

He shrugged. "I knew he was more afraid there."

Her mind refused to make the connection between the young man in the leather jacket and overalls sitting five feet from her and the bloody ruin of Anton's throat on the shore of the island. "Wasn't there another way?"

The flecks of gold glinted in his eyes. "If someone were trying to kill you and your whole family, what would you do? If you knew they would never, ever stop?"

How dramatic, she thought. "You'd do what you can, of course, but—"

"You'd do what you had to."

Even in the overalls, he didn't look quite as silly any more. She shifted her legs. "What's it like?"

"The same as taking down an animal," he said. "Did you want details?"

She scowled. "I mean, when you...change."

His frown lightened. "It's just something I do. What's it like? It's like...

there's so much of the world and it's so interesting you want to see all of it, or smell it, or taste it. Sometimes it's hard to focus on one specific thing, unless it's really interesting."

"But..." She searched for the words. "How does it feel?"

Breaker raised an eyebrow. "It feels like putting on a different skin, becoming the other part of me. I don't know how to describe it."

"Is it still you?"

He glanced at the patio. "Shouldn't we be worrying about the hunter?"

Valerie waved. "He's not going anywhere. And he's not coming in. I find if I'm trying to solve a problem, it helps me to focus on something else. Besides, if I know what powers you have, maybe that would help."

He snorted. "I'm not a super-hero. I turn into a wolf, I turn back."

"And you can only be killed with silver?"

Breaker rolled his eyes. "So, how that works. When we change shape, any wounds we have don't persist."

"They heal?"

"Sort of. I mean, every time we change shape, we change to a healthy body. But silver poisons us and stops us from changing."

Valerie remembered the ugly rashes around the arrow wounds. "Can you die from the poisoning?"

He nodded. "If it stays in long enough. Those arrows he was shooting... they had some kind of spell on them to keep them stuck in." Distaste flickered across his face.

The carpet was still wet where it had been cleaned, just at the tips of Valerie's fingers. She pulled them back. "I remember. And the moon..."

"You have a bond with the moon," Breaker said. "Many women do, because of...you know, the, uh..."

"My period?"

He looked away. "Yeah. So, uh, some women can connect with the moon when they're...around one of us. It's...I don't really understand it. But I can smell it."

"When you're a wolf?" He nodded. "What does it smell like?"

He laughed, shortly, and now he looked at her again. "It smells like warmth and flowers, like a garden in spring, except not. I don't know how else to describe it. I'm not good with words, really."

"Is that why you came back? Because I'm a...moon...daughter?" She rested a hand on her hip, trying to feel the tingle she'd felt when she'd called the moon, as if there were something inside her she could touch.

But she felt ordinary, the same as she always did. There was nothing flowery or garden-like that she could detect.

He shook his head once, then seemed to regret his quick response. "No. I came back…I knew you'd be in danger. I wanted to help."

He avoided looking at her as he said it. She groped for some way to avoid asking him directly about it. "Are there a lot of women like that? Moon-daughters?"

"Well," Breaker said, slumping back against the chair, "you're the third this season. The other two…"

"The two girls who got killed?"

He nodded. "You heard about that."

"From Leon." She tilted her head. "He doesn't like you much."

He shook his head. "Feeling's mutual now."

"Now?"

"Yeah, he said some shit."

He was staring angrily at the carpet. "I can't *imagine* you said anything back," she said.

Unexpectedly, he got up and walked to the fireplace, standing in front of it. "Have you thought about a way to get out of here yet without getting shot?"

"We could go out through the fireplace," she said, and he snorted.

"And ride away on our sleigh?"

She'd said it as facetiously as he'd responded. But the idea of going up and out triggered another thought. The memory of the night before swam in front of her eyes. "I wonder," she said slowly, "if this cabin has a basement."

They found a locked door just next to the linen closet. Breaker put his nose to the crack and nodded. "More than just a closet."

Ten minutes of searching didn't turn up any keys that fit. "I'll get it," Breaker said, and before Valerie could call from the bedroom for him to stop, he'd set one foot against the door frame, grabbed the door handle, and yanked hard.

The door came open with a screech of wood. Valerie rushed into the hall just in time to see the door frame sagging away from the wall, the lock wrenched out in a splintered mess. "Oh God," she said. "You can't just go breaking down locked doors."

"You'd rather just walk outside into arrow range?"

Valerie moaned, touching the broken door. "Martin's going to kill me."

"That your ex?" Breaker swung the door open and leaned into the dark space beyond, sniffing. "Not much down there. Some appliances. Wine."

"Wine?" Valerie came up alongside him, looking down the stairs. "So that's where he hid the good stuff. Bastard."

Breaker led the way down the stairs. "So did he just come up here without you mostly?"

"Martin's my boss." Valerie glanced back at the broken door. "He loaned me this cabin 'cause he wasn't using it."

"He probably wants to sleep with you."

She stopped on the stairs and stared at the back of his head. "How do you know that?"

"Letting you use his land, his private retreat. And he knows you're not married any more?"

"Of course." She hurried down the stairs to stand beside him. "Wait, how do *you* know?"

He grinned at her and tapped his nose as he flicked on the light. "You messed up your last name when you told me, and there's no recent smell of any man on your car, just an old one. But you're still wearing your wedding ring." He looked away from her, around the basement. Beside a large wine rack stood a wine fridge, and next to it a small freezer. There wasn't any other furniture down here, not even a rug to soften the concrete floor. On the other side of the wine rack, a doorway led further into the basement, or hopefully out.

"Hm. Martin's been holdin' out on us." Breaker had lifted the lid of the freezer.

Valerie came over to look. Inside were several neat piles of butcher paper-wrapped packages, inscribed "FILET" and "PORTER" on one side, "SHOULDER" and "LOIN" on the other. "That's from Vic's." Breaker pointed to the "SHOULDER" side. "Venison. The other is steak. Nice stuff. Not cheap."

"Well, to be fair, he didn't tell me I could have any food while I was here. It was just a place to stay."

"Bullshit." Breaker picked up one of the packages. "When you're a host, your guest has the right to anything in the house."

"Put that back." Valerie took it from him and replaced it. "I never heard that rule. When you're a guest, you have to abide by the host's rules."

Breaker grinned mildly at her. "We had different upbringings."

"No shit." She walked to the doorway and peered through, into a small, dank room illuminated by a small shaft of light from a grimy window. "Can you see a way out from here?"

She'd lowered her voice upon seeing the window. Breaker matched her tone. "There's a window."

"I see that," she snapped. "I meant a door."

"What's the matter?" He turned to her. "We'll fit through there. Less likely he'll be watching a window than a door."

She looked down at her (Karol's) white shirt, the jeans she'd been wearing since yesterday. "Let me get a change of clothes."

Five minutes later, she returned to the basement with a neatly folded shirt and jeans in one hand to find Breaker peering out the dirty window. "I don't see him anywhere out there," he said. "I'm not sure I would, though."

"If he was able to shoot at you on the patio, he'd be on the other side of the house." Valerie held out her hand. "Give me your jacket."

He started to protest, then glanced at the window and took his jacket off sullenly. In just the overalls, he looked like a reject from Hee-Haw, minus the straw hat. "Not one word," he said at her expression.

"Promise." She folded the jacket with her clothes into a neat bundle, forcing herself to suppress the giggles that kept threatening to bubble up from her chest.

Breaker fiddled with the shoulder straps of his overalls, at which point she had to turn away to stop from breaking out laughing outright. If he noticed, he didn't say anything; the next sound she heard was the creak of the window opening, slowly. She got control of herself and walked around behind him as he peered out. "No sign," he said softly.

She couldn't see anything but bushes and trees, either. "What do we do once we're out there?"

"Lake shore. We can walk around most of the way and stay under cover."

"Most of the way to where?"

He put one hand outside the window. "My place. Just follow me. It'll be safe."

"You'll keep me safe, will you?" she said rather more sharply than she'd intended, as he pulled himself through the window, pausing to look around outside.

"You don't need me to keep yourself safe. I'll just show you the way. Now shh." She was treated to a nice look at his rear end, and then he was out of sight.

She watched the window, smiling at his words. She could take care of herself, couldn't she? She'd beaten that other wolf, whatever it was. And if Karol showed up, well, he'd just better watch out.

Breaker's hand reappeared in the window and beckoned her forward. The caked grime and mildew from the window frame got all over her hands as she pulled herself up. She hated to lower her midriff onto it, and pulled herself the rest of the way through as fast as she could, landing on dry, dusty ground with sparse grasses all around. Immediately, she grabbed her pile of clothes and then, like in a spy movie, pressed herself back against the house and looked around.

Just ahead of her was a dirt path, leading from the front to the back of the house and, she saw, down to the lake. Beyond the path, low decorative plants had been invaded by taller weeds; she saw Queen Anne's lace and milkweed, familiar foes from her gardening days, and others she didn't recognize as easily. Bushes rose beyond them, wild and untamed, and then there was the forest, from whose shadows a large black wolf was padding.

She started to say something about the overalls, and then saw the white patch on the paw. The determination with which the wolf was coming toward her, the flat set of its ears, and the lowered head all snapped into focus. "Shit," she managed to spit out, scrambling to her feet and running toward the back of the house, down to the lake. If Breaker had gone anywhere, it would be down there.

The wolf angled to cut her off. Then she passed the deck, and from the dark crawlspace underneath, another black shape shot out to intercept the first. Valerie pulled up and turned in time to see the two collide, her pursuer faltering as Breaker slammed into it and knocked it to the ground. It yelped, or maybe he yelped in excitement as he lowered his jaws.

But the fight was far from over. The other wolf, Valerie saw now, was larger and had the advantage over Breaker in close quarters. It got to its feet quickly and, even though Breaker had his jaws around its neck, was able to swing him around and loosen his grip.

No, no, no. She had to help him. Valerie searched for something, anything she could use as a weapon. And then she heard footsteps coming slowly around the patio.

She ducked back into the crawlspace before she could think. The slow, measured pace of the steps told her who it was as clearly as if she could see his white suit. She groped around in the damp darkness while her eyes searched the ground ahead of her.

The footsteps stopped out of sight, off to her right. There was nothing in sight that even remotely resembled a weapon. A smooth sliding noise, like an arrow sliding out of a quiver, came from where the footsteps had stopped. Then her fingers touched an old, splintered board. It felt good and heavy when she picked it up. Perfect.

In front of her, the wolves were still grappling. Karol's voice barked out a command in some Slavic tongue. Valerie dragged the board out from the crawlspace, watching the larger wolf freeze and then start turning, trying to put Breaker broadside to Karol's bow. Breaker struggled against the other, but slowly was dragged around.

Karol was only ten feet from her, his white suit glowing in the sunlight, bow drawn and fixed on the wolves. His eyes flicked in her direction as she emerged holding the board. "Thank you," he said. "You should stay out of the way now."

"Like fuck I will." Valerie wound up, putting her body into bringing the board around.

He released the arrow, but she didn't see where it went. All she saw was him trying to use the bow to block the board. It snapped, and his arm behind it snapped as well. He roared and staggered, then charged toward her, murder in his eyes.

A black blur leapt from the grass and seized him by the throat. This time, Breaker held on as Karol went down, snarling viciously, pulling and tearing. Karol howled in pain, pushing ineffectually at the wolf, blood staining his suit jacket and shirt.

Valerie looked away, and saw the other wolf limping toward them, an arrow sticking out of its hip. She brandished the board at it. "You stay where you are or you'll get a mouthful of this."

It stopped and glared malevolently at her. They stood like that until Breaker said, behind her, "Let's get out of here. We only have a short time 'til he comes back. Don't turn around," he added hastily, forestalling her, "unless you really want to."

She didn't take her eyes off the other wolf. The arrow she'd plunged into its chest was gone, without a trace. "What about that?"

"We can outrun it. I'll be wolf. Just follow me. I'll keep you safe."

"Breaker," she said.

His reply was deep and guttural, part animal. "What?"

"Thanks."

A warm hand landed on her shoulder, a hand whose calluses were growing into thick pads, whose fingers shortened as the hand slipped from her back. She turned to see the black wolf trotting past Karol's body. Keeping her eye on the other wolf, she backed away. She couldn't resist looking at Karol, and immediately regretted it. The torn throat was as gruesome as Anton's had been, but that wasn't the worst part. The worst part was that Karol's was slowly knitting itself back together.

Chapter 10

She dimly registered the discarded overalls in the bushes as she ran after the wolf, down to the lake. No sound came from behind them, but she kept turning back to look over her shoulder as she stumbled across the rocks. The waves of the lake lapped at the rocks, and the world around them was so still that if her heart weren't pounding so quickly, Valerie would have thought it incredibly beautiful, exactly what she needed. As it was, all she could think was that there was nobody around to see in case Karol or his wolf jumped out, or came up behind them.

Breaker seemed unconcerned by any of that, perfectly in his element. He trotted along the shore, and though he almost never looked back to make sure she was following, he did stop and wait on the one occasion when she tripped and almost fell. After that, she noticed that his ears flicked around constantly, but mostly stayed back in her direction.

They walked for hours, it seemed, until her legs ached. She kept looking over at the lake, but the growing clouds must have scared the few tourists in the area into staying close to shelter. They extended out over the lake now, which provided welcome relief from the sun beating down on her head and neck.

Twice she thought she heard pursuit behind them, but when she turned, there was nothing there. The wind was picking up, though, and now there was almost a constant background noise of leaves. Waves from the lake lapped more strongly at the rocks, splashing up now as she skipped around them. To her left, the length of the lake stretched out before her; they were running around the south end now, leaving most of the resort buildings behind. "How much farther?" she called to the wolf ahead, knowing he couldn't answer.

He stopped and jerked his head forward with a short "arruf," and then kept going. She had no idea what that meant. Serves me right for asking a stupid question, she thought.

And what did she think she was doing anyway, following this wild creature deeper into the forest? All she knew was that the guy trying to kill him was a nasty piece of work; that didn't make him automatically trustworthy. Taking her back to his place, he said. She wondered for a moment if she would walk in the door to find the decaying corpses of the other two girls after all.

You have to trust your instincts sometimes, she decided, and when she was with Breaker, she felt as she had when driving through the maple forests, when kayaking out on the lake. With him, the world felt full of possibility; scary, but *right*. He wasn't Karol, who lived with one foot in a world Val couldn't see, nor Steven, whose confined world had drifted away from hers like a soap bubble on a summer evening. She didn't actually mind how much longer she ran with Breaker. Karol was behind them, the breeze off the lake was cool, and the air was clean and fresh.

It was only about another half hour before Breaker cut to his right, watching to make sure she was following. At first she thought he'd just run into the woods, but as she drew even with him, she saw a faint dirt path leading between the trees. She hesitated, looking back at the houses she could see on the west shore of the lake, and the untamed wilderness on this side. Breaker barked, his eyes gleaming in the shadow of the trees. She nodded, turned, and ran under the trees.

The clouds had already drawn shadows across the day, so when she jogged under the canopy of leaves, it almost felt as though she'd stepped into twilight. Breaker was an indistinct shadow ahead of her, but she never lost sight of him, even when she had to swat bugs away from her face constantly. They were much thicker here than they'd been by the water, or maybe it was the growing oppressive humidity driving them down to the ground.

With the bugs distracting her and Breaker to keep an eye on, it wasn't until he paused atop a large rock to lift his head and sniff the air that she realized that there hadn't been a trail to follow for some time. There wasn't much in the way of plants on the ground, though she noticed clumps of bushes here and there. She walked up beside the big black wolf, his head above hers now, and said, "Are we almost there?"

His answering "whuff" didn't really tell her, but when she followed the direction he was looking, she saw through the trees a wall of stone. Breaker jumped down from the rock and trotted in that direction. As Valerie followed, she saw the roof over the wall, and an incongruous satellite dish atop the roof, partially hidden by a nest of branches and dead leaves.

Breaker slipped through the open door of the cabin. Valerie started to follow, then realized he would be changing. She ran her fingers along the wall instead, tracing cracks in the old stone. Moss covered some of the stones near her, giving the whole building an overgrown, abandoned look, which she supposed was what Breaker wanted.

Around the far corner, a wider trail led away from the lake, in the opposite direction from which they'd come. Tire tracks were visible, leading off into the woods.

"Great location," he said behind her. "Equal distance from the lake, the road, and the pack."

She turned. He'd thrown on an old flannel shirt but hadn't buttoned it up, so it hung loosely over his jeans, showing off his chest. "Middle of nowhere," she said.

He nodded. "Hard for the hunters to find. Took the first one three months."

"Anton?"

"Was that his name? That one?" He jerked his thumb back toward the lake.

She nodded. "His brother is Karol."

"I sort of figured that. They dress pretty much the same."

She saw the matching gaping wounds in their throats. "If he brings the body back to shore, will it regenerate?"

Breaker shrugged. "I tossed it in the water last night. So I don't think it'll matter."

Valerie sighed and sagged against the wall. "So what now? I was going to just get out of here."

He looked off into the woods. "I was sort of hoping you might stick around."

She felt a small flutter in her stomach. "Really?"

"Yeah. You can call the moon. That might help get rid of the hunter."

Her head sank. "Oh."

Breaker coughed. "Uh, also, you were great back there."

The flutter returned. "I couldn't let him shoot you. After you saved me from that other wolf."

He growled. "That wolf tasted wrong. It's not natural."

"He made it to look like you."

"Well, yeah." He moved closer to her. "You know, it's probably not safe for you to go back to that cabin. If you want to stay here, I'll go get your stuff tomorrow morning."

When she looked up at his brown eyes, they were serious and concerned. "You'd be okay with me staying here?"

"You can't go anywhere else." He scratched his temple. "I don't mind. I mean, it's kinda my fault. It's just sorta messy inside. Don't get many visitors."

Valerie rolled her eyes. "I lived with messy for ten years."

"That long?"

"Married two years out of college." She sighed.

He leaned against the wall beside her. "It's hard when you think you know someone and it turns out you don't."

"What did you think you knew about me?" She looked down at her ring finger and rubbed the base.

"I could smell the moon on you. And no husband."

"So no surprises."

He shook his head. "My nose doesn't usually lie. Well, not this one." He tapped his nose.

Valerie played back her memory. "When did you sniff me? With your other nose, I mean."

"That first night you arrived."

Her eyes widened. "Wait. While I was out on the deck?" He nodded briefly, looking uncertain. "That was *you*? You scared the hell out of me!"

Breaker fidgeted. "Sorry."

"Sorry? Jesus, don't you know better than to sneak around in the middle of the night around women you don't know?"

He glanced sideways at her. "Leon said you had a husband. I was curious."

She felt the flutter in her chest again, stronger, turning her angry energy to something else. "Are you that curious about all women?"

"I'm a curious guy. It's one of my many flaws."

"Curiosity is the sign of a healthy mind and imagination," Valerie said.

Breaker snorted. "Not to everyone."

He looked so angry that Valerie felt a pang of guilt at having left his jacket behind at the cabin, because it would have looked so much better on him with that expression. Though he wasn't that young, his tone was that of a sulky teen, so she reached out in sympathy. "Your parents?"

"Pack." He shrugged. "Same thing."

"My mom can be stubborn, too. Like...she hasn't approved of one guy I've dated since I was seventeen," she said.

"What?"

"I mean, parents don't always know best. Right?"

He considered that. "I dunno. You're not still with any of those guys you dated, right?"

She brushed her hair back over her ear. "That's not the point." She lifted her head to say more just as he raised his hands to cup her chin and bring her lips to his.

Her surprise lasted only a few seconds. She put her arms around him and leaned up into the kiss, parting her lips. The wildness in him was a frightening, feral energy that flowed from him to her, sparking her spine and legs. She stood on tiptoe, pulling herself against him as his tongue played across her lips.

His hands slid down her shoulders to hold her closer. Her breath came more quickly, and now she could definitely feel his interest, not just in his warm breath or the tightness of his grip, but in the warmth pressing into her through his jeans. She wasn't even aware of the chill of the wind any more.

When their lips parted, he looked seriously down at her. "What would your mom think about me?"

"She'd hate you," Valerie breathed. "She's prejudiced against werewolves."

He laughed. "I get that a lot."

"A lot?"

"Well, more lately." He dropped his hands from her shoulders. "I don't usually tell women about that."

"Don't see why." Valerie rested her fingertips against his chest. His hair was thick, but soft. "It certainly sets you apart."

"It does that." He kicked the ground. "Want to come inside?"

The inside of the cabin was as messy as he'd promised. Clothes lay strewn everywhere, underwear draped on the corner of the television, jeans and shirts on the low, flat bed and crumpled on the floor. Wires from the television ran out of a small hole in the wall. The only surface that was clear of clothing was the motorcycle parked in the corner.

Breaker pulled a white t-shirt off the single wooden chair. "You can sit if you want."

"Thanks." The chair wasn't very comfortable, but it was great to get off her feet. Breaker didn't seem the least bit tired, pacing the room back and forth. She enjoyed watching him. "So what do we do now?"

He stopped in mid-pace. "I don't think we have to do anything for a little while. I have some ideas about how to deal with the hunter, but I want to talk to the pack first."

"No," she said. "I meant..."

He smiled. "Oh. I don't know. There's only really one place to go to dinner, and I'm not exactly welcome there nowadays."

"Does Leon own that, too? Or does everyone think you killed those girls?"

His smile vanished. He resumed pacing. "They can think what they want."

"Don't they know you?"

"I thought so. Guess that don't matter. People are always afraid of us."

Valerie folded her arms. "So talk to them."

"What the hell do you think I did? I didn't have any idea what happened. They said it was wolf attacks. I told them none of the pack would do that, and they told me I couldn't be sure, so I told them to go to hell."

She weathered his outburst and looked back steadily. "But now you do know what happened."

"Got a pretty good idea."

"So go tell them."

"Fuck them." He spit the words out. "We've lived here for generations. A couple deaths and they all turn on us? Fuck them."

"So, what, you're just going to ignore them from now on?" Valerie kept going even though he'd opened his mouth to respond. "Listen, trust me, I know what you're going through. People you'd been working with—living with—for years suddenly betraying you. But you can't just cut yourself off from everyone who does one thing wrong."

"You got divorced." He stared accusingly at her.

"Yeah, well, Steven did a whole pile of things wrong," she said. "And anyway, he left me."

"Then your mom was right about him." He sat down on the bed. "You know, forget them. I don't need them. I just need to talk to the pack, get rid of the hunter, and then things go back to normal."

"Where is the rest of your pack?" Valerie asked. "Why've I only seen you? Aren't they out trying to get rid of the hunter too?"

He shook his head. "They never leave the packland. Live and let live. When I told them about the hunter, they said the town would never let him come here. Then when he came here, they said as long as we stayed hidden, he'd never be able to find us."

"He found you."

He grimaced, looking around the small house as though the hunter might be lurking in one of the corners. "That's because I'm reckless. I go out and try to find things out. I put myself in danger. I put others in danger."

"But you save them from danger, too."

"When I can."

She came over to the bed and sat beside him. The mattress, under the clothes, still had some spring to it. "You saved me."

He raised an eyebrow. "I had to. Otherwise you might've gone to his place again tonight."

She deflated, sagging back. "You know about that?"

"I saw your car there. What happened?"

So she told him about the first wolf attack. He winced when she said, "I thought it was you," and she saw the haunted look in his eyes, the memory of the other two women. She told him about the deep sleep, about the dream she'd had, about calling the moon for help, and there he stopped her, gripping her wrist, his eyes bright.

"She answered?" It was the first time she'd seen him excited as a human.

Valerie nodded. "Just like she did when I was with you. What's so odd?"

He grinned, squeezed her wrist, and let go. "It's not odd, it's just...I didn't know the moon would respond when one of us wasn't around. See, we're her children, so everything around us is amplified, sort of, where she's concerned. It's really cool that you have that connection."

"Cool?" She laughed. "It freaks me out. I mean, could I have used it at work to get my boss to stop being an asshole?"

The grin hadn't left his face. "She can't do everything."

She leaned in a little closer. "Could she tell me what to do about you?"

His nose almost touched hers. "Nobody's been able to figure that out yet."

She couldn't think of anything else to say. So she kissed him again. His hands sought out her hips, leaning in toward her, as his kiss grew more insistent. The taste of him returned, stronger than her memory, his breath warm and rich against her cheek. She thought she could sense the wolf in it, that strong animal musk he'd brought into the cabin after he changed. Her fingers slid below his shirt, along his rib cage to his back, where she pulled him against her, down to the bed.

It had been as long for him as for her, she guessed, breathless in the deep passion of the kiss. His body pressed close, crushing her to the bed while her hands pressed into the lines of his back, hungry for more. His hips shifted, grinding his urgency against her thigh, at which point he lifted his head and propped himself up on his elbows, looking down at her.

"We don't have to go to dinner," she said softly, and reached down for her shirt.

He unfastened his pants while she was lifting her shirt off, turning his attention to hers while she was undoing her sport bra. Here in the cabin, with the clouds closed in overhead, the lighting was dim enough to be called romantic. The door was open, which was exciting even though she knew nobody would walk by to see them. She discarded the bra without hesitation, turning her bare chest to Breaker.

He trailed his fingers up her stomach and around one breast, then the other, while Valerie leaned back on her elbows and closed her eyes. His touch on her skin was exquisite, his fingers rough but his hands gentle, caressing rather than groping. Maybe it was her hunger that made it so good, that made each touch feel like it was drawing fire that lingered behind, but whatever the cause, Valerie breathed it in and reveled in it.

Then his hand cupped her breast. She felt his weight shift on the bed, his breath on her skin a moment before his tongue brushed her nipple. "Ohh," she moaned. "Don't bite me."

He paused. "Don't worry about that," he said softly, bending back to her. She sank back onto the bed, bringing her hand up to his stomach as he circled the areola and then pursed his lips over her again. She pressed up, her fingertips finding the ridges of his abdomen, exploring downward to the waist of his jeans, where she discovered that he hadn't bothered to put underwear on again.

His hips tensed as her fingers found the edge of his pelvis, content to slide along there and the powerful muscles beneath. He lifted himself across her body, brushing his lips across her other nipple, bringing his belly button under the heel of her hand. Fine hair, as thick as fur, met her questing fingers, and then, his hardness, warm and solid. Her body shivered then, a tug of his lips sending sparks through her, tensing her fingers around him.

They slid easily out of their pants, leaving them to join the others on the bed. She started to sit up, but he pushed her back, brushing his nose down her stomach to her sex. He was breathing in the scent of her, she realized, but not quickly or offhandedly; he was savoring it as one might breathe in the smell of an apple pie just out of the oven. It made sense that smell was important to him, of course. She brought his pants to her own nose, to get his scent, and was overwhelmed by the masculine animal of it, mingling with the cool, humid forest air coming in through the door.

He straddled her, smiling down. She lifted her shoulders to kiss him, reached down, and guided him into her.

It was as natural as if they'd been making love for years, like it had been with Steven once—no, Steven had never held her like this, arms clenched on either side of her while he drove into her. Breaker didn't hold back, but he held her so that, even though he was on top, she was a part of the experience, pulling her chest against him, dropping his lips to meet hers; Valerie, gasping, arched her hips to bring him deeper inside, lifted her knees to rub against the solid mass of his thighs.

Outside, the weather rumbled, or else it was Breaker's chest growling with his ever-more-fevered breaths. Valerie felt her own body tingle, her arousal burning hotter in waves, mounting higher and higher. Breaker crushed her to him, thrusting deep into her, his hips meeting hers and drawing back, quicker and faster until her waves crested and her body sang with heat and passion.

It went on and on, through Breaker's loud moan and clenched teeth, past his shudders and her own guttural cries. Even after they'd collapsed to the bed, panting, she felt the echoes of her climax singing faintly through her. She turned her head from one side to the next, resting on a pair of Breaker's jeans. As close and messy as the cabin was, it was more relaxing and enjoyable than Martin's neat, expensive lakeside house.

On the roof, the soft patter of rain came, hissing outside through the leaves. She couldn't tell whether it had started while they were making love, or just after. The sound complemented her exhausted, happy mood. Breaker was smiling lazily, eyes half-lidded, with a little of the playfulness she'd seen in him as a wolf. "Nice," he said.

"Better than nice." She rested her fingers on his wrist. He turned his palm upward for her to draw her fingers across. Whether it was the tension that had built up to this moment, the novelty, or just Breaker himself, Val felt light and warm, almost floating on the surface of the bed.

"How about 'great'?"

"That works." She looked around the cabin again. "You don't have a bathroom here."

He pointed toward the open door. "Biggest bathroom in the area. Fully recycling, too."

Valerie rolled her eyes. "Do you at least have toilet paper?"

"Not really." He rested his hand on her stomach. "Usually I just change before I go."

Valerie frowned. "Do you shower, or bathe? Or do you just magically become clean when you change?"

He raised an eyebrow. "Sometimes I take a dip in the lake for fun. Or to swim across."

She glanced at the light outside. It was definitely dimmer than it had been. "Is it past seven?" He frowned, not understanding. "I thought we could stop by Leon's, maybe get something to eat. I don't see a fridge here, either."

His hand pressed on her stomach as he got up. "I don't have that, but I do have some drinks." In the corner of the cabin behind the TV, he lifted a solid board and reached below it. "Beer? Or Coke?"

"Beer." He straightened with two beers in his hand and brought them over to the bed. She sat up and took one from him, holding it for him to prise the cap off with the opener. It wasn't cold, but it was cool and refreshing, and nicely hoppy. She gulped down half of it and set it on the floor.

"I guess you usually hunt for your dinner." She grinned.

"Sometimes. Rabbit gets boring after a while. I like a good cheeseburger as much as the next guy." He wiped his mouth. "Want me to rustle you something up? Might take a while in the rain."

She shook her head. "I don't do raw game animal 'til the third date."

He laughed. "Well, if you don't mind holding on the back of Fenris there," he gestured to the motorcycle, "there's a good burger place about an hour ride away."

Her stomach growled. "After I clean up," she said, and then touched his chest again. "And after I watch you change again."

He got up from the bed, the wolfish smile firmly on his face. Standing in the center of the cabin with the soft background noise of the rain, he faced her and lifted his head again. The change happened more slowly this time, or perhaps it only seemed that way now that she was expecting it. The hair on his chest and stomach thickened while the hair atop his head shortened. He grew a beard on his chin as it lengthened and pushed forward, but it was more than a beard; it kept growing up around his cheeks and over his nose. His arms twisted and legs buckled, his ears grew pointed and large, there was too much for her to watch any one area for more than a few seconds before something else drew her attention. The most interesting part of him grew stiff and hard before disappearing into a furry fold of skin to become a canine sheath.

When he'd dropped to all fours, he padded up to her. His head came up nearly to her chest when she was sitting down. Up close, he was enormous, but his eyes were the same: brown with gold flecks that caught what little light there was and danced with it. She cupped his enormous cheeks in her hands, fingers pushing through the soft fur. "I don't know why I'm not more freaked out by this," she murmured.

Breaker the wolf grinned. He pushed his head forward, touching his nosepad to her cleavage, and then exhaled warm breath over both breasts. "That doesn't help," she told him.

His eyes stayed fixed on hers and she could swear he was smiling. "All right," she admitted. "It kind of does."

He lifted his head as she lowered hers. She couldn't quite bring herself to part her lips, but she did brush them against his, and he seemed happy with that. He backed up and trotted to the open door, then looked over his shoulder at her.

"Go out in the rain?" As soon as she started to get up, he bounded out, disappearing around the right hand side of the cabin.

She paused in the doorway, putting her hand out in the rain. For a moment, she thought of work, her friends in the city. *How was your vacation?* Oh, great. I fucked this guy I barely knew, who turned out to be a werewolf, and then I ran around naked in the rain. It was like Woodstock. She laughed.

The rain felt good as she stepped out into it, a little chilly but not bad, washing away the sweat of her run and of their lovemaking. She took a few steps around the right hand side of the cabin, to that corner and around it, and then almost fell when a wet black wolf nosed his way between her legs, turning his head up to grin at her. "I'm cleaning up," she told him, and he bounded away again.

The lake was too far for a proper bath, and the rain too light for a proper shower, but Valerie made do with her hands, cupping them to gather water, rubbing herself clean. Breaker reappeared periodically, more and more wet each time. He shook himself next to her, making her laugh. "You'd better not do that inside."

When she felt appropriately clean, she went back inside and looked for something to dry off with. She heard the wolf come in behind her, and turned to see his chest and back lengthening, arms and legs thickening, as his fur thinned and he stood up, dry and still smiling. "Don't have any towels," he said, apologetically. "This shirt's clean, though."

He indicated the white shirt he'd taken from the chair earlier. Valerie took it from him and dried herself as best she could. She didn't really want to put her clothes back on, but Breaker was already getting dressed, and she didn't have anything else to wear.

"Sorry about your jacket," she said.

He nodded. "I can run by there and see if it's still around. I don't think he'll still be staking out the house. Probably went home."

"What if he went out to the island?"

Breaker shook his head. "I can still feel him. If he goes to the island, I lose that feeling. That's how I knew the other one was there. He thought his brother would mask him, but I can tell them apart."

"You can feel him?"

He rubbed his chin. "You probably could, too. It's the moon. They draw on a dark moon, so I feel it as..." He paused. "Y'ever pee on an electric fence? Well, guess not. But it's kinda like that jolt, just here." He tapped his chest.

"Can he feel you, too?"

"Yup. Oh, he can't tell where I am. And I can't tell where he is. I just know when he's in the area." He waved his hand around, including the space outside the cabin.

"Handy. How would I feel him?"

"Call the moon," he said.

She stepped closer to him. "Can you feel me?"

He grinned and put his hands on her hips. She tilted her head up and gave him a kiss, happy to find it was as full of passion and energy as it had been before they'd made love.

"So," he said, releasing her and walking toward the bike. "Dinner?"

"Please." She followed him. "Do you have helmets?"

"Um." He looked abashed.

"Right." She tapped her head. "That whole 'can't get hurt' thing."

"I'll drive slow."

She sighed. "Well, I guess I can ride without a helmet. It won't be the weirdest thing I've done this afternoon."

"That's the spirit." He walked over to the bike and rested a hand on one of the handlebars. "We just have to be back in about three hours. I'll drop you off here if you don't mind staying."

Valerie frowned. "Where are you going to be?"

"Oh, it's Moonsnight." He pointed overhead. "Full moon. The whole pack gathers to commit ourselves to her."

They engage in their filthy rituals and dances. "Tell me," she said slowly, "are you particularly vulnerable during that time?"

He frowned. "Only if someone were to discover the sacred ground. But it is well hidden with the moon's help."

"That's what Anton was trying to discover on the island," Valerie said. "He was trying to see through the moon's magic."

Breaker leaned against the bike, looking beyond the cabin walls. "That might work," he said. "I didn't think of it, but it might work. But he'd have to be able to see beyond...even if he could call the moon like you do, though, he couldn't see it."

"Is there a tall tree, and a large white rock?"

He jerked as though she'd slapped him. "How did you know that?"

"He found it," she said. "He wrote it down. It was in his wallet when I found him."

"Fuck." Breaker slammed his fist against the wall. "If the other one found him...maybe he just took the wallet. I didn't even check. Stupid!"

"No, it's okay," she said. "I took the wallet. I got the paper out of it."

"You?" The anger and fear were melting out of his face. "Oh, thank the moon for you, Valerie."

She smiled, sticking her hand in her pocket. "It's right here...in my..." She stuck her hand in her other pocket, then in both the rear pockets. "It was. I had it. I put it in my pocket, I know I did." She looked up at him, growing fear mirroring his. "I stuck it in this pocket right here, right next to..."

The truth hit her all in a wave then, staggering. "Next to the arrow," she said. "The one I pulled out to stab the wolf."

Chapter 11

"We have to assume he has it," Breaker had said. They were racing through the woods on the bike, and even though there was a trail, Valerie's bones rattled with each bump. How would anyone get used to this?

Stupid, stupid, stupid. She'd been so clever, getting the paper, knowing what it meant, and then carelessly letting it fall out. Yes, she'd been under the jaws of a giant unnatural wolf at that point, but she should've seen it afterwards, should've noticed the scrap of white on the path. At least she should've checked for it later. She refused to think about the consequences. They hadn't talked about that part at all, once they'd realized, just hopped on the motorcycle and driven off.

He hadn't wanted her to come with him, but she'd been adamant. "If they won't listen to you, they might listen to me. I've been to his house, I've seen him talking to that wolf-thing. I've seen the creepy garden he keeps." He'd given in, mostly because she wouldn't get off the motorcycle and it was too slow for him to go as a wolf.

The paved road was much friendlier than the dirt path. Breaker accelerated hard once they hit it, making her tighten her hands around him. Out here in the open, the light rain stung as it hit her, and if she hadn't already been wet, she would have been much more miserable about it. But she couldn't even focus on how strange it felt to be riding without a jacket or helmet. She pressed her head against his shoulders and looked up at the sky, where the clouds hid the moon. Mother Moon, she said silently, please help, please help.

Fifteen minutes up the road, Breaker pulled off at another dirt trail. Valerie was bounced and battered again, under a canopy that at least kept them relatively sheltered from the rain, until Breaker pulled up next to a thick, spreading oak tree after another fifteen minutes. When she got off, he rolled the bike under the tree. "This way," he said, jogging down a path only he could see.

She followed, kicking her legs free of bushes and vines. The undergrowth here was thicker than it was down by her cabin. Looking down, she almost ran into him when he stopped, looking ahead at what seemed to be the same empty forest. "High Wind," he called. "I must speak to Storm Cloud."

Nothing moved. Valerie was about to ask who Breaker was talking to when a piece of the shadow ahead of them detached itself from the undergrowth and trotted back into the forest. Breaker sagged against the nearest tree trunk. "I don't think this will help. They're not going to change the ritual. They're not going to want to fight."

"You have to try," Valerie said. Breaker looked at the darkening sky and didn't respond.

Valerie didn't hear him arrive. The hair prickled on the back of her neck, similar to the feeling she'd had going up the path to the cabin, the first time she'd seen Breaker as a wolf. She turned.

Facing them from the forest, a wolf larger than Breaker, with silvery-grey fur, stepped forward silently. It—he?—lifted his nose in her direction, then locked eyes with Breaker. He was magnificent, with a noble arch to his neck and his tail held proudly up. Darker fur followed the line of his back down to the tail. He stepped past Valerie and then bowed his head, contorting into a now-familiar shape to stand on two legs.

"You are early," he said to Breaker in a deep, measured voice. His silver hair and beard stood out in the deepening shadow, as did his gleaming eyes. His skin, darker than Breaker's, melded well with the shadows of the forest.

Breaker bowed. "Storm Cloud," he said. "I have brought a maiden of the Moon."

"I'm not really—" Valerie started, then stopped and bowed, as Breaker had done.

"I can see that," the man rumbled without looking back at her.

"We have an urgent warning." Breaker took a breath. "The hunter...the hunter I told you about. He has learned the location of the Moonsground."

"That is impossible." Storm Cloud did not seem the least bit perturbed. He stepped back so that he could look at both of them.

Breaker lifted his head. "It is possible," he said. "He—his brother discovered it from the island."

"No human can pierce the moon's protection." Was it her imagination, or did the old man's eyes linger on her?

"He is not human." Breaker stepped forward. "You have to listen. He's not human. She saw him."

For the first time, Storm Cloud reacted, turning abruptly to Breaker. "Not human?"

Breaker turned to her. "Tell him."

Valerie took a breath. "He talks to wolves. Not wolves, but he's conjured this wolf-thing. And he put some kind of spell on me." Storm Cloud had turned his attention to her, his eyes so bright she felt as though she were under a spotlight. "He keeps a garden in his basement. Wheat, and corn, and...and he has these little ritual circles of stones and teeth that he puts trash into."

"Circles? Trash?" The old man's voice had grown sharper. "What trash?"

"My Starbucks cup. He picked it out of the trash, and I found it...and there were other things, a piece of green cloth and a lipstick."

"A conjuring circle," Storm Cloud said, slowly. "Calling a creature from the earth to hunt down a victim."

Breaker was staring at the ground. She heard him murmur. "Green cloth. Green dress."

"You are correct, Breaker of Ground. They are not human."

Storm Cloud stepped forward, his nakedness much more obvious now. Valerie couldn't look away from him, so she did her best to keep focused on his face, which was lined with age and worry. "What are they?" Breaker said as the older man approached.

"They are farm spirits. *Poleviki*, my father called them. Demons in white." He stroked his dripping beard with one hand.

"Farm spirits?" Breaker shook his head. "I've never heard of them."

"They come from Europe," Valerie said. "He did. The old country, he said."

"They are guardians of the land, but twisted and vicious. They were summoned by farmers to protect crops and cultivation, but they will happily kill people who show no respect for the land. And they despise us with a passion."

Valerie nodded, brushing wet hair out of her eyes. "He called you parasites."

"How do we fight them?" Breaker said.

Storm Cloud spread his hands. "We do not fight them. The land has brought them here. We move on, or we die."

"*What?*" Valerie said. Breaker just looked disgusted.

The old man motioned to the ground. "They have ties to the land, and they have corrupted the moon."

"They can be killed." Breaker clenched his fist, teeth bared. "I killed one, on the island. He died like a mortal man."

"Nevertheless." Storm Cloud sighed. "We will discuss the matter after Moonsnight."

"If we survive!" Breaker's eyes were wide. Valerie could feel the tension in his body, radiating from every muscle. "Don't you understand? He knows where the Moonsground is. He can find us there!"

"Then it is her will." Storm Cloud lifted his eyes briefly to his namesakes and the moon behind them. "We have lived long, happy lives. We knew she would call us."

"I haven't!"

"No." The older man looked directly at Breaker. "That is unfortunate, that the fault of the father should come to rest with the son. Therefore, I release you from the pack." He raised a hand, palm toward Breaker, in a kind of blessing. "Should you choose to return, we will welcome you; should you find your own path, may it lead you to good fortune."

Breaker growled, deep in his chest. "It doesn't have to end this way."

Storm Cloud inclined his head. "You do not know that."

They stood in silence. The older man took a step back, raised his hand again, and doubled over on himself until the silver wolf stood on the forest floor. Deliberately, he turned and paced back through the trees, disappearing into the shadow.

Unexpectedly, Breaker turned and looked past Valerie. "What about you? Are you going to go through with this too?"

She spun around and saw, arrayed behind her, a pack of five wolves, grey and white, standing attentively. The foremost one lifted her head (her? how did she know that?) and padded past Breaker and Valerie, following the path Storm Cloud had taken. The other four followed her, in single file.

"Stubborn old..." Breaker growled as the last one disappeared. "They'd rather just...give up."

Valerie nodded. "A…friend of mine's dad was like that. He got sick, and…the doctors said he just gave up."

"But they're not sick!"

"No," Valerie said. "But maybe they're tired."

"You don't know what you're talking about." He paced back and forth, wiping wet hair from his face.

"How old are they?"

He stopped. "I…don't know. They were born here, most of them."

His face was hard to make out. Only the glistening trails of the rain defined it for her in the dim light. "How old are you?"

"I'm a pup. Thirty-ish."

"Ish?"

"We don't celebrate birthdays." He wiped his hair back over his head. "What am I going to do?"

"Get out of the rain?" Valerie tried to smile when he looked up at her.

"I'm serious." He stalked back and forth from one tree to the next. "I can't get him out to the island. I can't fight him on land. You can't fight him. I can't just abandon the pack."

"But he released you." She put a hand on his shoulder. About to ask if he could just leave, she saw his eyes. The dripping forest around them made a softly pattering background broken by his harsh breathing. It had hurt him when Storm Cloud turned his back, and Valerie was reminded again of Steven driving off in the pickup with the signed papers. She clenched a fist. After all, this was partly her fault, her carelessness with the paper leading directly to undo all the work Breaker had done to defend his pack. "What can I do?"

"If I couldn't convince them…this isn't your fight. I won't put you in danger."

"Oh, spare me," she said. "I meant about Karol. Can I get the moon to confuse him, or something?"

He gave her a slight smile. "It's worth a try. I can't think of anything else to do. If anyone can do it, you can."

She reached for his hand, held it in hers. "Tell me what you can about Moonsnight. Whatever I know will help."

He nodded. "The night of the full moon, we have to be wolves. We can't change, and we can't leave the Moonsground."

"How long does it last?"

"From first howl to last howl."

"And how long is that?"

He shook his head. "I really don't know. We sort of lose track of time. Hours, at least. Once it was sunrise."

"What does it feel like?"

He raised an eyebrow. "How will that help you?"

"It won't." Valerie smiled. "I'm just curious."

"Did you ever see those shows on TV where the people fall in love for no reason at all?"

Valerie laughed. "You mean the Lifetime channel? Yeah."

"Well..." He squeezed her hand. "It's kinda like that."

They held hands all the way through the wet forest, back to where the bike was hidden under the oak tree. Breaker wiped it off as best he could, but when they were both seated on it, he didn't start it up. "I can't take you to the Moonsground," he said. "I just can't. What I can do is bring you close to it, and then you can do what you can."

"Is there somewhere he's sure to come from? Somewhere I can watch out for him?" She rested a hand on his hip. Even through the wet jeans, she could feel his warmth, his life.

"I don't want you confronting him. You should be able to talk to the moon from a distance."

"I'm not going to hide if he's going to be attacking you. I'll find another board if I have to."

He smiled then, turning to look at her, and brought one hand up to her chin. "If I were him, I'd be terrified of you. Can you ride a motorcycle?"

"I will not run away if he's threatening you." She stared back into his eyes. A strand of wet hair had fallen across his forehead, dripping across his cheek. She brushed it back.

"If it doesn't work," he said, "leave the fighting to us. I want you to take the motorcycle and go back to your cabin. Pack up your car and go home."

Go back home, away from werewolves and polavik-whatever and earth-wolves that took gashes out of her arm. Back to her empty house and her empty job and Martin and no Steven. And no Breaker. "No."

Breaker shook his head, slowly. "You barely know me. You don't know the pack at all."

"Exactly." Valerie squeezed his thigh where her hand rested. "I want to get to know you better."

He leaned in to meet her. Their lips met softly, cool rain on both of them warming as they pressed together quickly and then separated. "If we win, I'll find you, Valerie Michaels. I promise."

She shook her head. "That's not gonna be good enough. You want me to just go back home, not knowing, until maybe you show up one day?"

"You can't come to the Moongrounds," Breaker said flatly. "And you can't go back to the cabin. The hunter will come right there if he wins."

It was harder and harder to make out any features of the woods around them, but she could see him as clear as day. "I'll go to the island, then," she said. "I'll wait there for you every day for the rest of the week. And if he comes there, I'll kill him."

Breaker's eyes widened. She was surprised by her own vehemence, too, but she gave him a resolute nod. "All right," he said, and kicked the bike to life. "The island."

As they bounced along the dirt trail, Valerie closed her eyes against the rain. His warm scent and the smell of the forest surrounded her in a haze that made it hard to remember the world outside. The urgency of her task filled her awareness. If she failed, people would die. Perhaps a whole pack. She'd faced high-pressure situations before, but always in cases where to fail meant, at worst, losing an account for the company. She'd lived through that.

She could do this. To make up for her mistake, to get back at Karol for attacking her, for the wolves she'd seen in the forest, and for Breaker. And if she didn't succeed, she would at least avenge them.

It was completely dark when Breaker turned off the main road again. They went a little way off the road and then stopped. Breaker turned off the motorcycle light, but didn't get off. "I'll go on alone from here. Wait with the bike. You're sure you can ride it?"

Without a protective jacket? Or a helmet? Screw it. "Yeah."

Then he slid off the bike. She followed suit while he slipped out of his jeans and dropped his shirt to the ground. "Don't worry about those," he said as she stooped to pick them up. "Moon's calling me. Just come here."

She felt him through her wet clothes, growing hard as his arms locked around her. His lips met hers, his body tight, skin warm even in the slightly chilly rain. While they kissed, she slid her hands down his back, feeling the fur thicken under her fingers. The tail was just a nub when her fingers reached it, but it pushed and rippled like a live thing, extending stiffly out. She pulled back when fur tickled her chin, watching his smile stretch back into a wolf's grin, keeping hold of his hands as they thickened into paws, until she was holding the front legs of a large black wolf, whose brown eyes never left hers.

"I'll do everything I can," she promised him. His nose came forward to touch hers, his warm tongue washed her lips, and then he dropped to his feet and disappeared into the night.

Chapter 12

The rain slowed. She thought she was imagining it at first, but then she lifted her head and it was no more than a sprinkle, a feather touch on her face. The clouds above her were thinning, not yet parted, but light enough to show her where the moon was. "Mother Moon," she said aloud into the stillness of the night, "help me hide the pack from the hunter."

No tingle answered her. She'd thought it wouldn't be that easy. No, if she were going to stop him, it would have to be something more physical. She couldn't kill him, but she thought, given time, she could stop him. She cast around the area until she found a large, solid branch, and set it by the bike.

She didn't know when Moonsnight officially began. Maybe not for another hour or two. The moon was barely up over the lake. "Mother Moon," she said, "where will the hunter come from? Please, help your children."

For a moment, there was nothing, and she feared that the moon would not respond at all. She had just said, "Please," again when she felt a small spark in her fingertips, and the clouds moved overhead. They parted quickly and came together again, just enough to show a flash of silver light along the glistening wet asphalt, leading south toward the resort.

"Great." She looked down the road, pacing back and forth, worry gnawing at her. Was standing and waiting really all she could do? She'd put Breaker and his pack in danger, and he hadn't even blamed her for losing the paper, hadn't blamed her for running to Karol the previous night. He's just a good-looking guy with a bike, she heard in her head.

"Shut up, Mother." Saying it aloud made her feel better. Breaker was no Steven. She put a hand on the bike's handlebars. What if she went to meet Karol, intercepted him on his way here? He'd be surprised, and she might be able to hurt him enough to keep him away. The big branch was too unwieldy to carry, so she left it across the yellow line on the side of the road, as a marker in case she needed to come back this way. A few minutes of searching brought her a smaller branch, which she broke at the end to create a sharp point before sticking it through the belt loop of her jeans.

Of course, she had no jacket and no helmet, so she couldn't ride the bike, she told herself as she got on. Pure insanity. She'd freeze to death in the wind, if she didn't skid on the wet road and split her head open. Never ride without a helmet, never ride without protection, her instructor had hammered into her during her lessons.

The roar of the engine was almost deafening in the quiet of the night. Valerie felt her riding days come back to her, a distant memory, the patterns of movement like signposts in fog. Even when she'd been riding, her bike was newer than this one, but the controls were familiar enough. Would've been nicer if he'd had a new Beemer, but this would do. She revved it up and got it turned around and on the road. The feeling of the wind whipping past her unprotected head went from strange to exhilarating, and the rest was easy, as long as she didn't corner too fast.

Which she did, not ten minutes later, her confidence returning just long enough for her to take a bend a little faster than she should have. When the bike hit a slick patch, it skidded out from under her, across the black road and into the dirt shoulder. She got her leg clear in time and managed to leap free as the bike went sliding down into mud. Stupid, stupid, she told herself, wrenching it upright. Won't do him any good if you wipe out and kill yourself.

Still, worry and adrenaline kept driving her faster down the road. She took the curves more slowly, her confidence growing with each corner. After about fifteen minutes, she wondered when exactly she would run into Karol. She was halfway to the resort already.

And then she came around a curve and saw headlights. With the wind in her ears, she hadn't heard the engine, so she had very little time to react. Was it him? It looked like a pickup truck. She swerved closer across the road, and the driver drifted to his right to give her room. As he did, the moon appeared from behind the clouds again, showing her the gloss of a black pickup truck and the white shadow inside.

Valerie had little time to react or think. She swerved abruptly into his path, and he, out of reflex, cut the wheel hard to the left, sliding across the oncoming lane to avoid her. The truck skidded, bounced onto the shoulder, and with a loud bang, stopped dead.

She slowed the bike and turned it around, some fifty feet behind the wreck. In the truck's lone remaining headlight, she could see a huge oak tree leaning over the windshield in a tight embrace. The grinding of the engine trying to start came once, twice, and then fell silent. She eased the bike closer and then stopped as a white-clad figure got out, staggering slightly. He seemed very bright against the dark shadows of the forest, making his way around the truck to the road.

"Get out of here," she yelled.

One hand on the tailgate, he stopped to face her. He didn't yell, but she heard his voice clearly in the still night. "You do not have the power to banish me."

"I can sure as hell make your life difficult."

He laughed. "After we spent such a pleasant evening together? How unfriendly of you."

"You're the one who set your wolf after me." The longer she could keep him talking, the longer he'd stay away from the Moongrounds and the pack. "That wasn't very friendly either."

"Oh, he just wanted to get to know you better. In fact, he's quite missed you."

He smacked the tailgate smartly and then jogged up the road. She just glimpsed the quiver and bow slung across his back as he passed the light of the truck's headlight. Then a shiver of presentiment made her kick the bike into gear a fraction of a second before a large dark shape leaped from the truck bed, heading straight for her.

The bike leaped forward as well, directly at the wolf. Valerie wrenched it to the side, and then, as the wolf landed and reversed course, kept turning it. The wolf leapt again, close enough that she could see its gleaming teeth. She drove past it, dimly registering that she was headed back the way Karol had come. The only thought in her mind was to get away.

She'd thought the motorcycle would be fast enough to leave the wolf far behind quickly. After a few seconds, she risked a glance back over her right shoulder. The road behind her was clear, the wolf nowhere to be seen. She relaxed, and then happened to turn her head to the left. The shadow pattering beside her on the road was not hers.

Turning her head further showed her the gleam of shiny black eyes staring up at her, white teeth bared in a mocking parody of Breaker's happy grin. She jumped, sending the bike swerving madly, and felt an impact on the left side, behind her. Desperately, she wrestled with the handlebars, but the wolf slammed into the bike again, sending it careening to the shoulder with her beneath it.

This time, she wasn't lucky enough to get her right leg free. The bike landed on her as she was trying, sending a stab of pain through it and bending it unnaturally to one side. Oh, God, she thought, this is it, this is it. As hard as she could, she pulled out from under the bike and crawled toward the forest.

Teeth seized her left shoulder, biting down hard. She cried out and wrenched away as best she could. The wolf let her go, mouth open in a silent laugh. Valerie stared at it, waiting, but it didn't move, just stood and watched her. Slowly, she tried to get to her feet, then collapsed again when her right ankle buckled under her weight. The wolf swayed its head from side to side, still grinning that stupid grin, as if to say, *what a pity, what a pity*.

Valerie pushed herself backwards, and now the wolf started walking toward her, one step at a time, the white spot on its paw bright even though the moon was hidden. Otherwise, it looked almost exactly like Breaker.

Breaker, she thought, and suddenly felt the warmth of him as though he were behind her, holding her in his arms. He wouldn't be here to save the day, not this time. No, he'd trusted her to save him. And he believed in her, she knew that. More importantly, she believed in herself.

Her left arm stung where it had been bitten, was sore whenever she moved it. The shoulder muscles complained at every bit of strain. Her right ankle was useless. But as she scooted back, her right arm brushed the stick in her belt loop.

It was only a stick. But it was a weapon. She scooted back again as the wolf came forward, and the next time her hand brushed the stick, she grasped it and pulled it loose, using her body to shield the motion from the wolf. Act afraid, she told herself, and then laughed. Like that would be a big trick. She tried to get up again, this time putting the weight on her left leg and hopping.

The wolf seemed to think this was delightful. It pranced around her, herding her this way and then that, dodging whenever she kicked out at it with her game leg. She tried to close with it, but it danced away. The next time she kicked, it grabbed her sprained ankle, bit down hard, and pulled.

Valerie fell hard, on her side onto the muddy shoulder. She kept the stick under her, hidden, and didn't move. Come on, she urged it, come investigate. Come finish me off. She didn't feel any more terror, only a grim determination to finish this.

With every second, Karol was closer to the Moonsground. She wanted to roll over and attack the wolf, but it would just skip away from her again. It didn't have to finish her quickly. As long as she was kept away from Karol.

But her lying motionless was apparently less fun for it. Over the silence of the forest and the smell of mud, she caught its foul breath, though she still couldn't hear it walk. She could feel its presence now, though, in the still of the night, like a discordant note just below the surface of a symphony. Its nose pushed at her leg. With an effort, she stayed still. It moved up, sniffing at the blood on her shoulder from where she'd bitten it. She felt it draw back to lunge again.

With a cry, she rolled over, bringing the stick up. The wolf dodged, but not in time; she buried the stick beneath its ribs. For an instant, it looked horribly like Breaker, yelping and writhing, but unable to break away. Valerie pushed harder, bringing both hands to the weapon and ignoring the pain in her shoulder. "For Mother Moon," she said. "Take that, you piece of shit."

Both her hands jumped with an electric shock. For a moment, the stick felt like a metal dagger in her hands. The white spot on the wolf's paw brightened until it almost blinded her. She squeezed her eyes shut as the wolf's whine grew louder and deeper. A wind picked up, keening with the same note as though the wolf had summoned it. It roared past her ears as if she were still on the bike, and then, just as abruptly as it had come, it vanished.

The brightness was gone, too. Valerie opened her eyes.

Her hands were wrapped around a stick buried in a pile of dirt. At the edge of the pile, near her, was a small scattering of objects: teeth like fangs, and a silver ring.

All the adrenaline left her in a rush. She let go of the stick and sat back, panting, staring at the glossy black dirt. It smelled wrong, it smelled foul. She grabbed at the silver ring, getting a couple of the teeth with it, and hobbled to the bike, sticking the items in her pocket. Turning the bike around to chase Karol, she hesitated. He'd said, "you do not have the power to banish me."

You do not. So there was someone who did.

She had the feeling that she was on the verge of understanding something important. *Take your time, Val, take your time. Only not too much time, because you've already pulled two arrows out of your werewolf, and the third won't be as easy.* She closed her eyes. The first voice she heard was Breaker's, and then her memory crowded others in alongside him.

The police. They brought them here.

I grew up a farmer.

I love the land.

Back on the ol' farm.

They brought them here.

I go where the land is threatened.

And she knew. It was a wild hope, but it was the only one she had. Painfully, she turned the bike and got on.

It was hard riding without the use of her right ankle, but not impossible. She leaned on the forward brakes and rode carefully, even though every nerve in her body was screaming either in pain or in haste. *I can't go any faster, I can't go any slower.* She passed the wreck of Karol's truck, and slowed, but the land-spirit in white was nowhere to be seen.

Just around the south end of the lake, the road flattened out, in a wide scenic curve that almost came right to the lake shore. When she could spare a glance to her right, Valerie saw the wide, long surface of the water rippling with the wind, distorting the clouds and giving the landscape a surreal air. She shuddered and bent over the handlebars.

The grocery was long closed, of course, but there was a light on upstairs. She looked for a door, and then in exhaustion just leaned on the bike's horn. Nothing happened, for so long that she started to wonder whether Leon and Annie had left the lights on and gone out. But then she heard a slam around the side, and Leon strode around the corner of the store brandishing a shotgun.

"Take your damn party—" He stopped short, staring at Valerie, then at the bike. He took another step and squinted. "Valerie?"

"Leon." She got off the bike on her left foot and almost fell. Leon lowered his gun and hurried to support her with his free arm.

In the light of the street lamps in the parking lot, she was sure she looked worse than she felt. Blood was running down her shoulder and there was mud all down her front, in her hair and on her face. Her hair was nicely wind-styled, though at least that had blown much of the mud and water out of it, and it was now a fairly dry cloud of tangles. There were probably other things Leon could see, because he looked at her as though she'd just turned into a wolf herself. "What happened to you?" he said. "Whose bike is that?"

"I need your help." She knew enough not to mention Breaker's name just yet. "Please, can you come with me?"

He eyed the bike. "On that?"

She exaggerated the pain from her ankle, not that she needed to much. "I was hoping you could drive."

Skepticism warred with concern on his face. "I wouldn't ask if it weren't important," she said, and he sighed.

"I'll get my coat," he said. "You be okay here?" She nodded. "Will I need my gun?"

She glanced at it. "Maybe. Yes."

"Hold onto it, then. I'll be right back."

She leaned on the bike until he got back, trying not to worry about every second that ticked by, trying not to imagine Breaker lying on his side with a silver arrow through him. When Leon came back out in his jacket, a navy blue windbreaker with the North Face logo on the front, a short, round woman trailed behind him, her hair tied up atop her head, wiping hands on her jeans. She pulled Leon to her and kissed him, quickly. "You be careful," she said, releasing him, and then, "Evening," to Valerie.

Valerie raised a hand. Leon took his gun back and raised it to show the woman. "I'll be careful, Annie."

He slipped his arm under Valerie's shoulder and helped her to the passenger side of the brown pickup. Inside the cab, it was almost warm, and the seat was soft. She sank into it and gave a happy sigh.

Leon got in quickly. "Sorry about the mess," he said, pulling the door closed and starting the truck. Annie stood in the headlights, waving as Leon backed out and drove to the parking lot exit.

"It's fine," Valerie said. "Turn left," because Leon had his right blinker on, preparing to head up the west shore.

"Thought you were staying at Martin's place." He turned the truck left onto the slick road. Water hissed under the tires as he accelerated.

"The trouble's not there," Valerie said.

He took his foot off the gas. "That was Breaker's bike," he said, in a sudden burst of realization. "I ain't goin' anywhere near—"

She put her left hand on his knee, holding her bloody shoulder with her right. "Please," she said. "He's going to kill them."

"You shoulda known that when you got involved with him. You know what happened to the last two girls he got close to?"

"Not Breaker—the hunter."

His expression melted into pity, lines making him look older than he was. "Sweetheart," he said, "that's what hunters do."

"He's going to kill all of them." She felt him start at that. "Not just Breaker, not just one bad one. The whole pack."

Leon stared out the windshield. "Maybe it's for the best," he said. The truck was coasting now. He gave it just enough gas to keep it moving.

"They lied to you, Leon. Anton and his brother."

"Never met his brother," Leon said, but he pressed down on the gas. Valerie felt the acceleration.

"They hate werewolves." She leaned closer. "They killed those girls. Not Breaker. Not one of the other wolves."

Leon shook his head. "You weren't here. They were wolf kills. I seen enough to know."

"You've seen enough. Seen them here? From this pack?" She watched him to see how sure he was in his conviction.

"Course," he said. "They brought deer around once a year for a while."

"Never attacked people before, though, did they?"

He spared her a sideways look. She hadn't lost his sympathy yet. The bloody shoulder was no doubt helping. "Listen, Valerie. I appreciate what you're trying to do. But really, you don't know—"

"Did they kill people?" She pressed her hand down on his knee.

"No," he admitted. "But we always knew it was a risk."

"And so you were ready when the hunters came along and staged it. All set to blame the pack. You see my shoulder? You know what did that?" She angled her shoulder forward.

He glanced, then looked longer than perhaps he should have. The truck scraped the side of the road. Leon jerked it back, giving it still more gas now. "Jesus," he said. "We're taking you to a hospital."

"No. Keep going." Valerie released his knee and sat back. "It was a wolf that did this. A big black wolf."

He didn't respond right away, staring ahead in the silence of somebody deciding whether to tell someone else something important. At last, he said, "I thought you knew about that."

"I do. I've seen Breaker change. This wasn't him. It was a...a...a fake wolf. The hunter made it out of dirt." She dug in her pocket, leaning back in her seat. "Dirt and teeth and this."

He looked at her hand, which held the silver ring and the dirty teeth. "Okay, don't be offended, but that sounds crazy."

Come on, Val, sell this. You've sold crazier shit than this, and this is actually the truth. "Crazier than werewolves?"

"Heh." He snorted, but looked uneasy. "That's different. They just always been here."

They were already a third of the way to the Moongrounds, or more. "And you don't care if they get wiped out."

"Look," he said, taking one hand off the wheel to wave at the road ahead, "I'm gonna take you where you wanna go. You don't hafta convince me you're doin' the right thing."

She sat back and chewed her lip. Leon drove almost casually, leaning back now, disinterested. She'd dragged him out on a chilly, wet night, and he was the only one who could help her, and all he was thinking about was how fast he could get back to Annie. Annie, in her shirt and jeans, wiping her hands. Annie, caring enough to come down to see him off. Annie, sending him off as Breaker'd sent her off, with a kiss and a prayer.

Valerie sat up in her seat. "You don't know how much he regrets what he said."

Leon frowned slightly. "Which thing?"

Valerie picked her words carefully. "The fight. Over the girls."

"Sure he does." Leon's demeanor didn't change. "Reckon he'd prefer not to've admitted to killin'."

"Did he admit it? Or did you just infer he was admitting it?" Her heart beat faster. She hoped Breaker hadn't actually said he'd killed the girls.

"He didn't deny it," Leon said.

"Maybe he was just too shocked you'd even think it was him."

"Oh, what'm I supposed to think? Girl comes in, says she seen a wolf, Breaker tells me he's talked to her, next day wolf kills her. Like you say, we don't get wolf attacks. I tole you, sometimes a mutt just goes bad."

"Breaker didn't go bad," Valerie insisted. "He's trying so hard. He's doing so much."

At that, Leon jammed his foot on the brake. The truck screeched to a halt. "You gone sweet on him," he said, turning to look at her.

Valerie stared back. "Yeah. So what if I have?"

"Just like them other girls. He could charm his way outta a snake pit, that one." In the reflection of the headlights, Leon looked disgusted, but Valerie thought there was a little admiration there, too.

"So why didn't he try to charm you?" He didn't answer, thinking slowly. "Leon, he saved my life. Karol came after me with that creature of his, and Breaker attacked it. He didn't owe me anything." She held out the silver ring and the teeth again. It wasn't strictly true that Breaker hadn't owed her anything, because she had rowed him away from the island, but he certainly hadn't had any obligation to come save her.

"I know I've only been here a couple days—Jesus, it seems like a month—but he's had plenty of chances to kill me. Plenty. So why would I be here defending him, pleading with you to come help me save his life, if he were really as bad as you think?"

"Coulda been someone else in the pack done the killin'," Leon said, reluctantly. "He just said..."

"What did he say?" Valerie pressed, acutely aware of every second ticking by.

Leon sighed. "I said maybe we oughta do something about them wolves before they killed more people. He said, you think I oughta do something, that's what you mean. And I said, if you're the one needs to do something, you go do it. And he said, fine, you want me to do something, I'll do it."

"Okay..." Valerie wasn't sure how to say it, but she was tired and she hurt all over, and she'd just about used up her reserves of tact. "And from that you got that he was a killer?"

"Was the next week the second girl died," Leon said. "I saw 'im after that an' told him we was thinkin' about gettin' help if he couldn't control his own. He grinned at me, a mean grin, an' he said, you do what you want, it ain't gonna make a lick o' difference." He smacked the dashboard with his fist. "But it *did*! We told Anton t'go to work, and there ain't been no killin' since!"

"Because that's what they wanted!" Valerie felt her excitement matching his. "They needed you to invite them here. They can't attack the pack otherwise. The protection's too strong."

Leon didn't look at her, just clutched the steering wheel in both hands. Then the truck's engine roared, and it leaped forward onto the road.

They passed Karol's pickup. "Look out for a big branch on the left," Valerie told him. "Across the white line." She craned her neck to see if the pile of dirt that had been a black wolf was still there, but showing it to Leon wouldn't have accomplished anything anyway. She doubted that even a farmer would look at a pile of foul-smelling dirt and say, ayup, that ain't from around here, reckon your story 'bout demon hunters is all true, miss.

She saw the branch before he did. For a while she'd worried that Karol would have kicked it away, that he would somehow have realized that it was a marker. But it lay there, exactly as she'd left it, pointing into the woods in the direction Breaker had gone. Leon pulled the truck off the road and stopped, leaving the headlights on. "You sure it's here?"

Valerie opened the door. In the still night, she heard the howling of wolves. "Positive."

In her fatigue and haste to get out, the pain of her sprained ankle just one of many her body was shouting about, she'd forgotten it wouldn't bear her weight and had to grab the rear view mirror to stop herself from falling. "Easy there," Leon said, hurrying around to steady her. "How are you going to get up there?"

She looked at him as if he'd asked her to drive his truck into the lake. He got the point without her having to speak. "Whoa, I thought...I thought I was just driving you here."

"I need you," she said, gritting her teeth against the renewed surge of pain in her ankle and shoulder, even though Leon was supporting her on the other shoulder, "to get rid of the hunter. Come on."

She hopped forward. Fortunately, he came with her. "Wait, get rid of him? How...I mean, there was a whole room full of us..."

They couldn't tell where the howls were coming from, but Valerie could see a stand of pines ahead of them, tall, jagged shapes against the dimly lit clouds. She guided Leon toward that, the effort taking most of her breath over the uneven brush. "You...farmed the land...you have a... connection...to it."

"But I still don't see—" He broke off as a yelp cut off the howling, loud in the night. Stillness followed.

Valerie pushed forward even harder, and Leon stopped arguing. He half-carried her up a hill, and then they ran as though they were in a three-legged race. The yelp had definitely come from ahead of them, near the pines. They'd only made it halfway to the trees when a second yelp sounded through the night. Now they could hear running and movement, but only faintly over the sound of their own footsteps through the wet underbrush.

Ahead of them, a glimmer of white. Valerie slowed Leon down and pointed to it. He nodded and then called, "Hey! Hunter!"

Valerie winced. "Are you crazy?" she whispered.

Leon shrugged. "Why do we need to sneak up on him?"

By the time Valerie decided she couldn't think of a good answer, they had gotten close enough to get a good look at the white thing. It was not Karol; it was a large rock streaked with white quartz, taller than she was. "Damn," she said, but they kept walking toward it anyway. "Anton's notes said something about a white rock. I guess this is it."

Indeed, from the rock, they could see down a small hill into a clearing. The stand of pines marked the far end of the clearing, which at first appeared to be empty. Valerie leaned against the rock, letting Leon go while she stared harder down into the open space. There, to the right, she saw a silver shape lying prone. Near it, the slightest of movement. Silver, not black. She kept searching, until Leon touched her hand. "There," he said, pointing. She peered around the rock to see what he was looking at.

Like a ghost, a tall white shape hovered behind a tree just in front of the pines. It was the tallest point on the hill that overlooked the clearing, so it was clear why he'd chosen it. Valerie looked from him down the slope of grass, but the bottom was dark, full of brush, and she couldn't make out any shapes or movement there. Her gaze returned to the silver shape. She could now make it out better: a large grey wolf. It could be Storm Cloud, or it might not be. A smaller shape near it, darker, was nosing at the prone shape.

"What are you doing here?" Karol sounded testy. Valerie leaned against the rock. He hadn't seen her yet.

"Just came by to watch you work," Leon said affably. "We hired you, after all."

Karol didn't respond immediately. Finally, he called, "You've disturbed my quarry."

"Sounded like you shot a couple already." Leon's voice remained neutral. "Thought there was only one killer."

"There were two deaths," Karol said. "Where there is one killer, there are more."

"You sure about that?"

Their voices rang out in the still forest, unnaturally loud. Valerie's heart pounded. She fingered the silver ring in her pocket and wanted to ask the moon what to do, but Karol would possibly (probably?) be able to detect that.

"You hired me to do a job," Karol called again. "Pray leave me alone to complete it."

"What if I told you the job's done?" Leon said, sharper. "What if I told you a city girl did for your killer wolf already?"

The silence that followed that question was oppressive. Valerie clutched the ring and waited for Karol's answer. When he did respond, his voice came from closer than it had been. "I would say, let the young lady come out from behind the rock and accuse me herself rather than hiding behind an innocent farmer."

The silver ring slipped from her fingers, down into her pocket. She reached for it again but somehow couldn't find it. Well, it wouldn't prove anything anyway. Steadying herself with her right hand, she hobbled around the rock. "All right, here I am. You killed those girls, and then you set your wolf on me. How do you like that?"

Karol shook his head. He'd slung his bow back over his shoulder, she saw, and his right hand was curled into a fist as if he were about to hit her or Leon. "You're a bit distraught," he said. "After you were attacked by the wolf, you came to my house. I took you home the next morning and didn't see you again until you nearly hit my truck this evening." He said those last words with some venom, then smoothed his voice down. "You told me you'd been attacked by the wolf again, you were ranting that it was my fault somehow...I think you may have hit your head when your bike fell. You really should wear a helmet, you know."

Leon had turned to look at her. She cried back to his doubt, "He's lying! He set the wolf on me. It came out of the back of his truck."

"Tch." Karol smiled. "You are welcome, of course, to inspect the truck bed for any sign of wolf. But the black wolf that attacked you did not come from there. I think we all know where it did come from."

His right hand opened abruptly, empty. Valerie stared stupidly. "That's...that's not what happened," she said. "Leon, you have to believe me. Breaker didn't—"

A part of the shadow below her came to life, as if the darkness itself had spawned it. In what was becoming a horribly familiar scenario, it was on her in a moment, before Leon or Karol could react. She screamed as she went down, feeling the hot, foul breath of the earth-wolf as it lunged for her throat and missed, teeth sinking instead into her injured shoulder.

"It's here!" Karol cried. "Keep back, I'll dispatch it."

It's not Breaker, Valerie wanted to scream, he can't leave the Moongrounds. Don't you know that? Of course, Leon didn't know that; he thought it was Breaker attacking her. She tried once again to warn him, but her breath was precious, needed for struggling against the heavy shape atop her. Its teeth slid down her shoulder, inching closer to her throat no matter how hard she tried to push it away. It didn't growl, it didn't make any noise at all.

"Hurry!" Leon yelled. But Valerie knew that Karol wouldn't fire his shot until she was dead. She pushed harder, fingernails clawing at the wolf's face. It turned to snap at her hand, barely missing, and then

and then there was a concussive impact, something like a rocket exploding next to the wolf just above her, and its weight pulled her to one side, then released her. She clutched her shoulder, pushing herself back along the ground. Leon was at her side in a moment, staring with her at the bizarre sight.

Two black wolves wrestled on the ground, one with a white spot on its paw, the other black all over. No, Valerie moaned, it'll kill you. But Breaker was holding his own and more, his jaws fastened on the other wolf's neck. The earth-wolf rolled over him, and still Breaker held on, struggling free and shouldering his enemy to the ground again. The earth-wolf curled and kicked, and Breaker swung out of the way.

They were moving so quickly it was hard to keep track of which was where. The earth-wolf flailed more and more desperately, Breaker dancing around to avoid his attacks. Valerie saw again the flash of white on the earth-wolf's paw and spun to see Karol not two feet from her, bow drawn, arrow poised.

"No!" she screamed, pushing off with her one good leg and leaping into him. He dodged, but the arrow slipped from its string and fell to the ground.

Leon rushed to Valerie's side as Karol glared down at her. "That's gratitude," the hunter snarled.

A choking sound came from behind them. Leon and Valerie looked at the struggling wolves, Breaker now on top of the prone earth-wolf, whose front legs were struggling feebly. Breaker planted his own feet and pulled, tearing out a huge black chunk of the other's throat.

And what had been a large black wolf with a white spot on its paw crumbled again into black, foul dirt. Breaker spit a mouthful of dirt onto the ground and glared at Karol.

Leon was glaring at him now, too. The hunter looked feral, furious. "Do not act in haste," he said.

Valerie held Leon's wrist. "Do it now," she said. Breaker growled assent behind them. *Mother Moon*, Valerie said to herself, *bless us*.

The hand that held Leon's wrist tingled. Leon didn't give any sign that he'd felt it, but he reached down to the ground with his other hand and scooped up a handful of dirt. Staring up at Karol, he let it trickle out of his fingers. "Get the hell out of here, and don't come back," he said.

Karol shuddered, taking a step back. Valerie could feel him resisting, as if someone were pushing against her through the air. This won't be enough, she thought, but it's all we have. It has to work. She felt Breaker behind them, adding his resolve, and tightened her grip on Leon's wrist.

Karol wavered. His shape seemed to fold and crumple. "You will regret—"

He never finished his sentence. As if he were a leaf, his form skidded backwards on the breeze, disappearing into the trees. In a moment, he was gone.

Chapter 13

Valerie sagged backwards, almost collapsing as the earth-wolf had done. But her fall was stopped by a firm furry shoulder, propping her up as a warm muzzle pressed against her cheek. On her other side, Leon had grasped the hand that had let go of his wrist. "Valerie, you okay?"

Next to her ear, Breaker growled. "It's okay," she said to him. "He came here and helped." The stillness of the night felt more peaceful now, less ominous. She was able to relax.

Leon stared past her shoulder at the wolf. "I don't think you killed anyone," he said.

Breaker's growl faded, but only a little. He moved, and Leon removed his hand from Valerie's. Only then did Breaker quiet.

Valerie rested her head against his. "Silly," she said. "Don't be jealous."

He huffed onto her neck and then pressed his head against her shoulders, trying to lift her. "I'm so tired," she murmured.

"She's done a lot too," Leon said. "She can rest."

Breaker kept pushing, now making a soft whine. The sound told Valerie as effectively as words what he meant. "Oh," she said, and struggled to stand. "There's wounded wolves...I have to remove the arrows."

"Why do you have to do it?" Leon helped her stand, though she saw his reluctance.

"I get help from the moon," Valerie said.

With Breaker on one side and Leon on the other, she made her way down the hill. At the bottom of the hill, Leon stopped. "I...can't go any more."

Valerie felt the slight tingle as of an electric fence, but she knew it wouldn't hurt her. "I can make it," she said, leaning heavily on Breaker. With his help, she hopped to where the silver wolf was lying.

A smaller brown wolf next to him looked up hopefully as they approached, but Valerie could see without crouching down that she was too late to help. The arrow was buried in the large wolf's chest, and not even the faintest motion of breathing was visible on its sleek pelt. As she stood beside it, the clouds parted so that the moon shone down, and the body's outlines blurred. Valerie wiped her eyes, and they resolved again.

"I'm sorry," she said. Breaker bumped her gently, then led her onward. The going was easier with the ground illuminated, silvery tussocks and patches of mud with fresh wolf tracks that Valerie avoided, out of courtesy or superstition. They came upon a shadow beneath a bush whose eyes shone with the light of the moon. Valerie could see the shaft of the arrow protruding from its side.

Breaker brought her right up to it, where she fell to her knees. That was the easy part, she thought, not looking forward to getting back up. But she was within reach of the arrow. She held it and said, through ragged breaths, "Mother Moon...help me...please help remove this..."

The arrow fell away into her hand. She sat back on the ground, and when she opened her eyes again, saw motion in her peripheral vision, a dozen wolves surrounding her. Arms circled her from behind, strong and warm. "Thank you," Breaker said. "Sleep. I've got you."

Thank *you*, she wanted to tell him, but her eyelids were so heavy and her tongue wouldn't move. She turned, but he said again, "Sleep," and so she did.

Sunlight washed over her. Her eyes felt gummed together, and when she raised her left hand to wipe them, pain shot through her shoulder. Setting the arm back down, she felt the bandages on it tugging at her skin.

"Easy there," an unfamiliar woman's voice said. Valerie managed to open her eyes and saw a woman on the far side of middle age, hair tied up atop her head. "Surprised you're awake. Finally convinced the boys to leave you alone and now you wake up."

"What...what day is it?" Valerie murmured.

The woman chuckled. "It's Friday, dear. You've only been asleep for five or six hours."

"Oh." Valerie tried to remember what day she'd been at the island, what day she'd run around the lake with Breaker. Her legs ached, but her ankle was immobilized and numb. She blinked to bring the room around her into focus. She saw Martin's 42-inch TV directly in front of her, a window beside it with the shade drawn, and it was through that shade that the sun was beating. "I'm at the cabin?"

"They brought you back here. Leon came and got me." She smiled. "I'm Annie. I don't think we met."

"I saw you last night," Valerie said. "We kept Leon safe."

"If only he'd done the same for you." Annie clucked. "Gettin' mixed up with the pack. He knows better. They leave us alone, we leave them alone."

"They bring you venison." Valerie didn't know where she'd dredged up that piece of memory, nor why she'd felt compelled to say it.

"Aye, that they do." Annie's voice was soft. "And it seems we should have put more faith in 'em."

"They made it look good." She meant the hunters, and Annie understood that.

"They did. But hush, you should rest a little more."

"I'm awake." Valerie struggled to sit up.

Annie stood and watched, then shook her head and helped Valerie up. "Good heavens, you're as stubborn as those boys are. Are you hungry?"

The hunger was a gaping ache inside her, like a dark circle in the center of the moon. "Starving."

"All right. I brought some eggs from the store, and some bread. Good thing, too. You didn't have much here worth making. I'll fix you something nice." She paused. "I'd ask if it's okay to let the boys in, but I don't think I could keep 'em out."

"Damn right," Breaker growled, almost pushing past her as she left the room. He sat down on the edge of the bed and rested a hand on Valerie's. "How you doing?"

"Been better." The sight of his untidy black hair, gold-flecked brown eyes, and sharp nose brought a smile to her face. "You?"

He shrugged. "In one piece. Glad you're okay." He grinned, brightening like the moon peering through the clouds. "We did it. I dunno how you knew to bring Leon, but it worked, whatever it was."

"It was the land." She caught movement out of the corner of her eye and saw Leon standing in the doorway. "Karol kept talking about his ties to the land. I was wondering why it was so important for them to frame you for killing those girls. It was so the people who farmed the land would invite them in, give them permission and…and power, I guess… to go after you. So I had to get someone with a tie to the land to revoke that permission."

"We shouldn't never have let 'em in," Leon said. "But it looked…"

"I know how it looked," Breaker growled, his smile gone. He didn't turn to look at Leon, but he had that fixed look that showed where his attention was.

"You coulda spent more time explaining yourself."

"I don't owe you—"

Annie called from the kitchen. "Leon! Come help me in here."

Valerie smiled as the tall grocer slapped the doorframe in exasperation and disappeared. Breaker returned his attention and smile to Valerie. "Some people don't change, eh?"

"Guess not." It was comforting having him there with her. She sighed. "How is…?"

"High Grass Running? She's fine." His brow lowered.

Valerie felt the drooping in his posture, in his hand on hers. "It wasn't Storm Cloud, was it?"

Breaker shook his head slowly. "It was Summer Breeze. His mate. Of all of us…all of them…we all loved her. She never said a word against me."

"I'm sorry." She knew how inadequate the words were.

Breaker nodded. "The rest of the pack is safe, though. And we're going to stay that way for a while."

"I sure hope so." She shifted, wincing as her shoulder twinged again. "You can't bite me so I can just heal, can you?"

"If it was that easy, there'd be a lot more of us." Breaker rubbed her hand with his fingers. "You don't want to be a werewolf anyway. It's messy. There's fleas."

"I could wear a collar."

The corner of his mouth twitched. "You get kicked out of the pack for that."

"I guess it would be kind of hard to explain at the nightclubs, too." She leaned back against the pillows, letting her gaze wander to the window, which was smaller than the TV. The sun had risen past the window, so she indicated it with her chin. "Can you open the shade?"

Breaker nodded. He covered the distance to the window in three quick strides, snapped the shade up, and was back at the bed almost before Valerie knew it. She could see the gleaming lake surface and the trees and sky above it. From the kitchen, the smell of eggs and toast wafted in. "So can a werewolf date a normal woman?"

"You're anything but normal," he said.

"I'm not a werewolf."

His fingers rubbed hers. "You're a daughter of the Moon."

"Okay." She smiled up. "Can a werewolf date a daughter of the Moon?"

He raised one eyebrow. "My father did."

Valerie absorbed that. "Who's your father?"

"Trail Finder."

She waited, but he wasn't going to say anything else. "I didn't meet him."

"No." When she kept her eyes on his, he said, "Can we not talk about my family?"

"All right," she said. "For now. But only because of everything you've just gone through."

"Everything *I've* just gone through?" he said, and then laughed, and relaxed, leaning over to kiss her forehead. "All right, all right. Don't worry about what the pack thinks. It won't be an issue."

"Because you helped save them from the hunters?" She saw that wasn't right from his reaction. "No?"

"You were there," he said. "Storm Cloud released me from the pack."

"Oh. I thought that was just a formality, a kind of, you know, save yourself if you really want to, but it wasn't serious..."

"Well," he said, "no. It was a little more serious than that. And leaving the Moongrounds, that was a lot more serious."

The import of that hit her almost immediately. "You left...to save me." He didn't react to that, but that in itself told her the answer. She turned her hand over to squeeze his. "Oh, Breaker..."

"Listen," he said. "Don't make a big deal of it. It was way past time I cut loose from them anyway." But he didn't meet her eyes as he said it.

"Oh." She looked out at the lake again. "Well, so what are you going to do now?"

He gave his trademark shrug. "Not sure. I guess now the pack's safe, I'll wander around. See a bit of the world."

And she, she was going back to the city, back to her job. The fight she'd had with Martin over the job was ridiculous to her now, both that she'd allowed him to overrule her and that she'd gotten so upset over something that was ultimately so meaningless. She was almost excited by the prospect of going back and confronting him. After a mystic hunter and a pack of werewolves, a puffed-up boss was nothing.

But the idea of Breaker losing his family and wandering alone gripped her heart. And more, the idea of going back to the city and not seeing him again gnawed at her. She couldn't fall for another man, not this soon, and certainly not a werewolf. She tried to imagine her mother's reaction, her friends' reactions. No, she couldn't do this.

She couldn't. But no matter how hard she told herself to release his hand, she couldn't do it.

"Maybe," she said slowly, "you could start with New York City?"

He didn't answer, but he squeezed her hand, just as Annie called, "Breakfast's ready!"

Val looked up. Breaker's expression curved slowly into a smile. He put a hand on her stomach, gently. "I hate cities. I'd have to have a really good reason to go."

"I know at least one thing there that doesn't exist anywhere else in the world."

His smile grew. "That might convince me. You hungry?"

She brushed a lock of hair from her face. "Starving," she said.

Chapter 14

It was strange walking into the office again. Her ankle was still tender enough to require crutches, but her shoulder had healed nicely. She stood at her desk and rested her fingertips on the notes she'd scrawled to herself before the meeting, two weeks ago. They were the salient points of her proposal. She had difficulty calling it to mind now.

Resting her crutches against the desk, she eased herself into her chair. The message light on her phone was blinking, but she ignored it. She put the box she'd brought on the floor behind her desk and waited, sipping coffee.

She knew it wouldn't be long before Martin interrupted her, but she thought he'd at least wait until his intern brought him his 10 am Starbucks. Wrong; it was 9:25 when he knocked on her door and let himself in.

"Hey there, Valerie," he said in that cautious, placating voice you used with invalids, as if he were afraid that greeting her normally would be insensitive. He plunked himself down in the chair opposite her desk and stared at the crutch. "Back on the job, huh?"

"Looks that way." She set her papers aside and folded her arms on her desk.

He cleared his throat. "So, uh, I went up to the cabin Friday night." He waited, but she just nodded and let him go on. "Where'd you go?"

"After the accident, I decided to head home," Valerie said. "I thought it would be more relaxing."

"Oh yeah, Leon said you rolled a motorcycle." He shook his head and did that forced-laugh thing. "I didn't even know you rode."

"Used to." She indicated the crutch. "Guess I should've practiced more."

"Yeah. So why did you break the door to get into the basement?" He was recovering a bit of his top-dog manner.

"Why did you go up to the cabin?"

Martin gestured with one hand. "It's my cabin. I wanted to get away. Been a really bad week."

"So you figured I could sleep out on the deck? On the couch in the living room?"

He didn't fidget under her stare, but he did glance away from her. "Sure. I mean, I didn't think much about that. But look, you broke a door, and that, that's going to cost some money. I got a guy coming out this week to do an estimate."

"Send me the bill," she said carelessly.

"Also for that wine you took."

Valerie narrowed her eyes. "Oh, there was wine missing?"

"Well, why else did you want to get into the basement?"

She stifled a giggle, imagining telling him the real reason. "I was just curious. And a little bored."

"You must've had a friend with you, someone pretty strong."

She pretended to consider that, shook her head. "No, that was just me. And I didn't take any wine."

Now he did fidget. "Well, it was irresponsible, that's all. Someone else might have broken in, and…if there's wine missing, I'll send you the bill."

"You do that." She sighed. "What do you want, Martin? I've got a lot of crap to catch up on."

"How did you drive home, with a sprained ankle?"

She grinned. "A friend drove me back."

He squinted. "You called someone to come up and drive you back?"

"No, someone I met up there. I've been showing him around the city the last week." She let him hear the word "him" very clearly.

"Oh." He seemed to slump down in the chair, then pushed himself to get up. "Well, welcome back. Team meeting at eleven, as usual."

"Oh, Martin," Valerie said as he stood. "I see we got Vodotech signed. I want that account."

He gave her that familiar smile, back on solid ground. There was a slight edge to his voice, a testiness that had only appeared when she'd mentioned a male friend. "Of course I will be interested to see your proposal—"

"That's not what I mean," she said. He looked startled that she'd interrupted, but she didn't give him a chance to protest. "I deserved the DivaCorp account, and you know I did. Now, unless you've got a daughter for Don to bang, too, I want Vodotech."

Martin's eyes widened. "That's inappropriate," he said. He started to go on, but under Valerie's stare, his words died out. "How about we discuss Vodotech over lunch?"

"Sorry," she said. "I have a date. But if you want to talk, we could talk about how inappropriate it is—not to mention creepy—for your twenty-nine-year-old director of marketing to be dating your nineteen-year-old daughter."

"They met at the Christmas party," he said, but feebly. "Look, I can't tell Julia who to date."

"You can sure as hell do a better job protecting her from people who are just out to look good to you. For Christ's sake, open your eyes."

He looked stricken, but only for a moment. "I'll see you at the staff meeting," he said. "Oh, and, uh, I'll forward you the details on Vodotech. You can submit your proposal by the end of the week."

"Thanks." Valerie smiled. "But I don't think I'll be submitting it."

"What?" That caught Martin completely off guard.

"And I'm not going to the staff meeting. I just came in to give you my notice. It would be two weeks, but, you know…" She waved a hand toward the window. "I really don't want to wait that long."

"But you're…I mean…look, Val, you can't just…" She watched him twist, trying to figure it out. "So you met someone. You can't just throw away seven years of experience…seniority…wait." He watched her start to throw her personal items into the box. "Did you meet some guy from another firm? Did he offer you more money?"

"Not even close." She wasn't worried about money, although in the back of her mind she thought maybe she should be. Her savings wouldn't last forever. But then again, look what twelve years of planning for the future had gotten her.

"Then what? A title? Another account? Look, you can have Vodotech."

She held up the picture of herself and Steven, held it over the box. Then she moved her hand and dropped it in the trash can. "I told you, Martin, I'm done with that. I'm done with all of this."

He straightened. His expression came back under control, reset to be neutral. "Fine. Clear your desk out by noon. I'll send someone up to escort you out."

"That's okay," Valerie said. "I've got my own escort."

She nodded toward the door of her office, where Breaker had sauntered up and was leaning. Martin whirled and stared.

"Morning," Breaker said, hands in the pockets of his leather jacket.

"This? This is the guy?" Martin turned to her and laughed. "Well, Val, when you get over your midlife crisis, don't bother coming to me for your job back. We are through here."

"That's what I've been trying to tell you." She smiled. "Good-bye, Martin."

Breaker's nostrils flared as Martin made a detour around him. "Hey," he said. "The girl you took up to the lake last month."

"W-what?" Martin stared at him.

"The one you slept with. She's the one who took your steaks. Don't blame Val."

Martin shook his head. "How can—"

"Breaker lives up there," Valerie said. "He hears things."

Breaker tapped his nose. "Lived. And I follow my nose. Just thought you'd like to know."

Martin looked back at Val, then at Breaker. "I am definitely calling security. You have five minutes."

"More than I need." Valerie waved good-bye as Martin disappeared.

"Charming." Breaker straightened and took a step into the room.

"Well, he's a boss." Valerie swept the rest of her things into the box.

Breaker came around the desk and smiled. "But not your boss. Not any more."

She shook her head as he picked up the box. "Thanks." She pushed herself out of the chair and stood on one leg, getting the crutches situated. Breaker leaned forward and kissed her, and she let that go on long enough that she was worried that was how security would find them before she realized she didn't care.

Either Martin had been bluffing, or the building security was slower than usual, because nobody bothered them on their way down to the lobby. Breaker threw the box into the back of Valerie's car and slid into the driver's seat, grumbling. "Can't wait to get back on my bike."

"It'll be ready tomorrow. Enough time for us to pack and head out. Where are we going again?"

He pulled the car out of the parking garage and into the sunlight. "Does it matter?"

Valerie closed her eyes and smiled. The engine purred below her and the sun warmed her face. Breaker's smell, beside her, was rich and masculine, and her leg didn't even hurt much anymore. "No. Not at all."

About the Author

Kyell Gold writes primarily anthropomorphic ("furry") fiction, and is most famous for his stories in a Renaissance-era world (***Volle, Pendant of Fortune, The Prisoner's Release, Shadow of the Father***) and his stories in a contemporary world (***Waterways, Out of Position, Isolation Play***). He has won ten Ursa Major awards for his novels and short stories. ***Out of Position*** also won the Rainbow Award for Best Gay Novel of 2009, and in 2010, his short story "Race to the Moon," published in "New Fables," was nominated for a WSFA Short Story Award. Other strange things he likes to write about include mystical decks of cards, superheroes, and sports.

He was not born in California, but now considers it his home. He loves to travel and dine out with his partner of many years, Kit Silver, and can be seen at furry conventions in California, around the country, and abroad. With his friend K.M. Hirosaki, he hosts a podcast about writing called "Unsheathed," produced by Kit, and although Kit and K.M. both enjoy a glass of wine, Kyell prefers Coke Zero to fuel his podcasting and writing.

About the Artist

Bay Area artist Kamui enjoys kayaking, romantic walks in the woods, and avoiding werewolf maulings whenever possible. Further examples of his work can be found at *www.furaffinity.net/user/kamui*.

Other Books by Kyell Gold

Volle - A fox spy in a foreign country finds the distraction of potential romance nearly fatal.

The Prisoner's Release and Other Stories - Short stories from the furry land of Argaea, following the novel Volle.

Pendant of Fortune - Volle returns to defend his honor and finds himself defending his lover as well.

Shadow of the Father - Yilon must take charge of a foreign land, and defuse species tensions between foxes and mice.

Weasel Presents - More short stories from the land of Argaea.

Waterways - Kory the otter comes to terms with his romantic attraction to another boy, which complicates his senior year of high school.

Out of Position - Dev, a tiger who plays college and then pro football, falls for Lee, a gay activist fox, throwing both their lives into turmoil.

Isolation Play - Following his public coming-out, Dev must deal with fallout from his team and family, and so does Lee.

Bridges - Hayward is great at setting up pairs of friends of his, but who will help him find what he won't admit he needs?

Science Friction - Vaxy is at the center of a gay erotic farce with his graduate school professor, his roommate, and their friend. Oh, and the professor's wife.

In the Doghouse of Justice - An anthology of the private lives of furry superheroes.

Green Fairy - Sol, a young wolf struggling with being gay during his senior year of high school, finds an old book that sparks dreams which change his life.

Find the most current information about Kyell Gold's works at *www. kyellgold.com*.

www.ingramcontent.com/pod-product-compliance
Lightning Source LLC
Chambersburg PA
CBHW071347170626
46811CB00003B/1023